FIGHTING LADY JAYNE

DIVINITY WARRIORS

MICHELLE M. PILLOW

MICHELLE M. PILLOW® - MICHELLEPILLOW.COM

Fighting Lady Jayne (Divinity Warriors) © Copyright 2009 - 2018, Michelle M. Pillow

Fourth Print Edition July 2018

Third Print Edition September 2017

Second Print Edition July 2012

First Print Edition May 2009

Second Electronic Printing February 2012

First Electronic Printing May 2009

ISBN-13: 978-1-62501-188-6

Published by The Raven Books LLC

ABOUT FIGHTING LADY JAYNE

DIVINITY WARRIORS BOOK TWO

Alternate Reality Romance

Jayne Hart has earned her independence by becoming Divinity Corporation's inter-dimensional boxing champion. Life is great, until a dirty fighter knocks her unconscious. Now, abandoned by the corporation in a parallel world, Jayne will use every weapon she has to be free once more. Even if it means running from her sexy new "husband" and spending the rest of her life in a primitive forest.

Ronen of Firewall longs for a woman to warm his bed and his home, but he had no intention of choosing a bride. In an unprecedented move, one chooses him. Never in the history of the marriage ceremony has a woman dared to lay claim. How can he resist the alluring Lady Jayne? She's confident and sure in her decision to be with him—until their wedding night when she's nowhere to be found. But, Ronen is not one to shy from a battle. He will find Jayne and, when he does, he has one particular "weapon" in mind for taming his seductive, wayward wife.

In a land forever at war, the Starian men are so busy fighting that their marriage ceremony has been reduced to a "will of the gods" event where they simply pick a woman out of a lineup and claim her as a wife. With women becoming scarce, it's necessary to trade the offworld Divinity Corporation for brides.

They live a very Medieval-like existence. Instead of medical advancement and technology, all of their focus has been on developing weaponry and battle strategy. With places named for war, such as Spearhead and Battlewar, these men have been left in charge way too long. They are in desperate need of a woman's touch.

.

The Playful Prince
The Bound Prince
The Rogue Prince
The Pirate Prince

✕

Captured by a Dragon-Shifter Series

Determined Prince
Rebellious Prince
Stranded with the Cajun
Hunted by the Dragon
Mischievous Prince
Headstrong Prince

✕

Space Lords Series

His Frost Maiden
His Fire Maiden
His Metal Maiden
His Earth Maiden
His Woodland Maiden

✕

Qurilixen Lords Series

Dragon Prince

Marked Prince

More Coming Soon!

✕

To learn more about the Qurilixen World series of books and to stay up to date on the latest book list visit www.MichellePillow.com

AUTHOR UPDATES

To stay informed about when a new book in the series installments is released, sign up for updates:

michellepillow.com/author-updates

PROLOGUE

GETTING her teeth knocked around in her head hurt like hell, but being able to spit blood into the face of her opponent more than made up for the discomfort. Jayne "The Sweet" Hart laughed as Big Bobby Bishop sputtered in anger. She knew he expected her to cry at the landed blow. Truth was, part of Jayne did want to cry. She wasn't a glutton for a beating, and that last hit had left blood running out of her mouth at a steady flow. They'd been going at it for nearly a half hour, bare-knuckle boxing—no protective gear beyond any sanctioned bioengineering, no referees, not like some of the other dimensions had. No, here on dimensional plane 241 almost anything was legal. That's why the gladiator ring paid such big money and drew the notice of rich, inter-dimensional travelers who could afford a private plane jump through Divinity Corporation. It's also why Jayne agreed to travel from her own world to this alternate reality where laws were more of a suggestion and killing someone in a fight was considered a good thing.

In many ways, each alternate reality was like drifting through time on her own home plane, had a singular event on the timeline been changed. Each dimension seemed to be a different outcome to a similar historical start. Some were so technologically advanced everything was done for them, and they'd found a worldwide peace and understanding. Jayne generally stayed away from those levels of existence. There wasn't much employment for fighters in such realities.

Other planes hadn't even developed a means of fast communication beyond throwing a bird into the air with a tiny letter tied to its leg. Still others had just installed their first aqueducts or invented their first vehicles to run without horses or oxen. Or, like 241, they had every technological comfort and yet somehow managed to maintain their barbarian sensibilities.

Any way you looked at it, Earth was Earth, just

different versions of itself—same languages, matching natural events, some people looked the same but weren't. Humans, for the most part, still resembled humans. And those with power were still greedy bastards trying to tell her how to do her job.

Big Bobby watched her expectantly, his mouth opened as if to scream in victory at any second. Jayne knew he expected her to fall with that punch. She watched as the excitement slowly died from his eyes, replaced by shock, then confusion, until finally a boiling rage. His eyes scanned the crowd before moving toward the large balcony to where his daddy sat watching. Big Bobby's father and known gangster boss had undoubtedly assured his halfwit-of-a-lug-nut son that he was a sure winner. It wouldn't have been so bad if Big Bobby had been an admirable opponent, but after a half hour, she could still see out of one of her eyes, and he only managed to knock her off her feet twice.

And Bossman Bishop wanted her to take a dive to this chump?

Jayne snorted. Not bloody likely. She'd never work as a boxer again—not that she had to. In her home dimension, she had plenty of money to bide her twelve lifetimes.

Divinity Corp paid her big for this fight. They

were her ticket home and had the only known source of inter-dimensional travel technology on this plane. Natural slips were extremely rare and the timing of them completely predictable by the company, even if they didn't know where the slip would go. If they didn't take her home, she'd be stuck until the end of time. Besides, there was no way she was taking a dive just because the local gangsters had promised to…

What had Bossman said again? Oh, yeah. They were going to gang rape her grandma while she watched. It had hardly been a threat. Jayne was an orphan. Still, a part of her was up in arms for the hypothetical grandmother they'd threatened.

There was no way Bossman could know about her lack of family. The publicity put out by Divinity Corp's entertainment division fostered the wholesome image of their Sweetheart Jayne. Of course, it was all a lie. They hired a family to take pictures with her at a rented country home—the devoted mother, the fake twin sister with a poor health condition, the baby brother and suit 'n' cravat dad.

The loud, almost fanatical cheering of the crowd grew. They surrounded on all sides, lining the rows upon rows of rotating theater seats. Every few minutes, the seats would shift, changing the angle from which a person watched. Lights flashed all around her. Floating cameras zipped by her head, but she ignored them. Most of the bets were on her and she never lost a fight. Never. And she would be damned if she gave this guy the reputation of being the one person who could take her down. He didn't deserve the title or her respect. Rage grew within her that he even dared to presume he was worthy of taking her down.

Do it for your family, Jayne, she thought sardonically.

Jayne decided to teach him and Bossman a lesson. She drew her body around, preparing to kick him upside the head in a move she knew he wouldn't see coming. Big Bobby swung again. She dodged the blow, and this time his hand merely grazed her cheek, stinging the cut she had there. She didn't hesitate. Whipping her leg around, she swung for his head. Suddenly, every nerve in her body exploded with pain. There was no stopping her body's momentum as it lifted off the hard mat. The noise of the crowd faded and grew until stopping altogether. Big Bobby caught her suddenly slowed foot and pushed her backward. Nothing was as it should be. Lights streaked in her vision before her body was abruptly stopped by a metal pole slamming into her back. Then, darkness clouded her mind and she could only think one thing.

Boxers' Poison.

1

JAYNE PERCEIVED the exact moment her mind became aware that something wasn't right. Her body didn't ache and her body always ached—if not from a fight, then from her workouts. The second hint that all was not well came in the form of her mattress. The thing was much too soft. She didn't sleep on soft things, *couldn't* sleep on soft things. Jayne had grown up in an orphanage. Where she came from that meant hard floor beds and a high pain tolerance from the daily obedience beatings.

Where in the bloody fucking misery was she?

She listened first, not moving, not changing her breathing. The soft whispers of others filled the space around her. People slept. The even tempo gave it away. Opening an eye, she glanced around and took quick inventory—dim light, stone wall, barred door, five sleeping women, not counting herself, on mattresses placed in various positions around the room.

Prison.

Jayne frowned. Her tank top and exercise pants must have been confiscated, replaced by a shapeless white, very one-size-fits-all, dress. She'd been arrested before, usually for disorderly conduct. Surely she'd remember celebrating her victory. Nothing to worry about. Divinity Corp always sent someone to get her out of jail. Ah, the perks of being a champ.

Wait, victory? Jayne shot up on her mattress. *Boxers' Poison.*

"Bloody fucking misery, son of a whoring cat..." Jayne cursed under her breath. A blonde head moved nearby, followed by a light whimper.

Jayne didn't care if she interrupted her neighbor's beauty sleep. How could that father of a monkey do this to her? Big Bobby had drugged her. His last hit had been tainted with Boxers' Poison. One punch to an open wound and down went your opponent. All fighters were supposed to have been tested for such tricks, as was protocol. Even on 241 it was illegal. What fun was a drugged fight to the crowds? Well, except for the drugged fights on plane 23.

"That flying piece of monkey dung," Jayne swore again, feeling the familiar urge to hit something ball up inside her. She wasn't sure what was worse—being cheated or having nearly four hundred dimensions that participated in the underground entertainment division of Divinity Corp think she lost to such a whoreson.

"Keep it down," someone mumbled. "I'm trying to sleep."

"You keep it down," Jayne muttered under her breath, unafraid of the warning in the woman's tone. Where was George, the Divinity Corp entertainment lawyer? He should be getting her out of there already.

A sinking feeling came over Jayne. What if George wasn't coming? Technically, she'd lost the fight. If Divinity believed her to have lost a fortune in assets, they'd...

"Oh, misery." Jayne reached for her face, not feeling a single swollen eyelid or bruised cheekbone. She'd been healed. That meant she'd been out for at least a couple weeks. Boxers' Poison didn't last that long, so someone had deliberately kept her under while they transported her to this cell. Management always joked that they'd make her disappear if she ever lost a match. She'd thought they were teasing. Someone always had to lose. Sure, it was never her, but someone had to. "Oh, bloody misery. They shipped me off. They made me disappear."

"I said to keep it down!" A dark-haired woman sat up, blinking hard. "What the...? Where?" Her gaze darted around the room in surprise, and she let loose a loud, long, hairsplitting scream. The prison cell instantly became a blur of jolting movements as the other women awoke. Jayne covered her ears, glaring at the woman who refused to stop her incessant yelling.

"Eh, what's all this noise?" A gruff voice yelled. A man who could only be their prison guard appeared in front of the bars. A burly man dressed in a hard leather jerkin and dark breeches stood between the bars and the stone wall on the other side of the narrow hall. Metal diamonds plated the leather of his clothes. He clanked a heavy metal weapon against the bars to make them ring. "Stop that. You woke me from a dead sleep. No talking. No waking. Lie down until it's time to break our fast. The next one to make a sound, I swear to the fire goddess I will run you through with my sword."

The woman stopped screaming, but her wide

eyes still yelled in silent terror. Jayne looked around at the rest of her companions. None were as silly as the screamer, but nearly all looked just as confused. All except a redhead who hugged her arms around her legs and rolled back down onto her mattress bed.

One of the two blondes whimpered and did as she was told, sniffling noisily. Jayne realized it was the same woman who'd been sniveling as the others slept. The second blonde appeared much calmer as her eyes met Jayne's. She didn't say a word as she took in their surroundings. The last prisoner, the brunette, scratched thoughtfully at the back of her head as she eyed the retreating guard.

"We'd better do as he says," the brunette said, only to add to herself, "for now."

Jayne silently, though reluctantly, agreed. There was no point in causing trouble until she knew what was happening. Pressing her hand against the hard stone of the floor, she slid the mattress aside. Though bumpy, the stiff bed was a cool relief to the softness. Threading her hands under her head, she closed her eyes. The only thing left to do was wait, for all would unfold itself in time.

✕

"THE FASTER YOU make them come, the less time you must spend in their presence."

Was this whore serious?

Jayne eyed the servant who'd introduced herself as Sera. At least, the woman said she was a servant. What kind of servant, Jayne wasn't sure. The woman had a white corset top, laced so tight it made her generous bosom nearly pop over the top of her shirt. Long blue skirts, a favorite accessory of most of the whores Jayne had met in her travels, billowed around her legs. They made for easy access to the professional tools.

"I'll make them do something, all right, but it won't be making them come," Jayne muttered under her breath, as she accepted a loaf of bread from the woman. The other women in the cell did nothing to acknowledge they'd heard what she said. Of course, none of them were really talking, not since the guard had come in the middle of the night to threaten them. Maybe if she yelled the guard would open the door to give her the fight she was brewing for.

Calm down, Jayne. It's like Coach Wagner used to tell you. Not everything is settled with fists.

To which she always replied, *Yeah, there's kicking, too.*

"That is all they want—a vessel to find release

in," Sera continued softly, her rounded eyes trying to convey her sincerity. Jayne didn't trust her. In fact, she didn't trust anyone, not completely. "Do not expect tenderness, but if you don't deny them, if you don't resist, you'll be treated fairly enough. And if you give them sons, you'll be greatly rewarded. Life here is not so bad."

"This isn't happening, this isn't happening," a dark-haired woman repeated, over and over. She only became more hysterical with each passing moment. "Wake up, Edith, wake up."

Jayne blocked the sniveling woman out of her mind and bit into her bread. There had to be a way out of the prison. If only she had something besides a white, shapeless gown to bribe the guards with.

"I'm telling you how to best survive this place. Please, listen," Sera insisted. "Spreading your thighs is easy enough a task for a decent life. Don't bring trouble upon yourself. Let them find release. They are not such boars when they get what they want."

Jayne hummed softly as the servant woman left them. Perhaps bribing with coin wasn't the way. Escape might be much easier. Edith became louder still and Jayne thought about knocking her out to put them all out of their misery. One of the blondes tried to soothe the hysterical one's fears while the other blonde whimpered. The redhead picked imaginary dust particles off her long sleeve, ignoring everyone.

Jayne turned her attention to the brunette, watching as she pulled a hairpin out of her hair. The woman didn't hesitate as she knelt down by the bars. Reaching through, she closed her eyes and slipped the tip of the hairpin into the lock and began to work it in small circles. Jayne bit her lip, leaning in to stand watch without having to be asked.

"Put it up," Jayne whispered, seeing a wooden door open at the end of the long corridor. Two burly men dressed in dark breeches and hard leather jerkins with the metal diamond-shaped plates strode toward them. Jayne slowly backed away from the bars as they came to stand in front of her. A warrior studied them one by one, not appearing pleased with what he saw. Jayne knew the feeling. She wasn't too pleased with him either. To the other guard, he said, "The flaxen one and the crying one. They do not carry themselves well. Take them and give them the philter."

"What?" Edith screamed. "No, wait! I'll be good. I swear I'll be good. Please, don't hurt me. Please, I'll do anything you want. Do you want me to make you come? I will. I swear I will. I'll do you all!"

Both guards snorted in disgust. Jayne resisted the

urge to thank them. With the two crybabies out of the cell, she might be able to come up with a plan. One motioned to the door and soon four men were crowding into the small place. Two grabbed the now-sobbing Edith and dragged her out. The blonde screamed, kicking and fighting as tears streamed down her face. The four remaining women held perfectly still.

After the men passed through the door, the brunette set back to work, her face set as she tried to feel around the lock.

"You won't be able to open it," the redhead said, staring at the lock picker. "Even if you did, there would be no escape. You'd have to fight through the warriors' hall, out of the guarded castle gates and run three strikes over open prairie until you reach the forest. Should you survive the wild beasts that live there, you'd soon find yourself prisoner to an even more vicious race of creatures—monsters so fierce and depraved they'll make you beg for death. Trust me, with the war going on in this forsaken place, we're in the better of the two sides."

"Who are you that we should trust what you say?" the brunette asked.

"Name's Paige," the redhead answered.

"Lilith," the remaining blonde put forth.

"What do they want with us?" Jayne inquired. All eyes turned to her. "Oh, I'm called Jayne."

"They want us to be their whores," Paige said bitterly. "They don't call it that, but that's what they want—a subservient woman to rub their feet and spread her legs. If you don't, they get pissed and the whole lot of them stares at you like you are demon spawn incarnate and blames you for your chosen warrior's bad mood. It's either fuck them or suck them or you're treated like the bottom rung of Starian society."

"Again, I ask, why should we trust you? We don't know you." The brunette continued to try to pick the lock. "You could be a plant sent here to make us behave with horror stories of what's beyond the tree line."

"I don't care if you trust me, but I know what I'm talking about. This isn't my first time in a cage." Paige tilted her head back and sighed. "They'll be coming to get us soon."

"What's your name, locksmith?" Jayne asked the brunette.

"Karre."

"Well, Karre," Jayne said. "I don't think we have much of a choice. If we all work together, maybe we stand a chance. Now, I don't know how we all got here, and at this point I don't think it matters, but I do know I'm not staying to spend the rest of my life as some guy's sex toy."

"I agree." Lilith stood. "We need a plan."

"Fine," Karre grumbled.

Paige opened her eyes and shook her head. "Don't look to me to join your little band. You're only fooling yourselves. I've been to the Hanging Forest. I made it all the way to the Starian borders and I've seen the creatures that wait beyond."

"What about a dimension jump?" Lilith inquired. "Does anyone know if this place has inter-dimensional travel technology?"

"A what?" Paige asked.

"Staria? It's too primitive. They don't have the technology here," Karre said. "I got a glimpse of the castle when they brought me to this cell. Through a door I saw servants cart water from a well in buckets and the drive wasn't paved. No artificial lights or motorized vehicles. Though there were several large horses."

"I've never been here," Jayne put forth, "but I'm inclined to agree from what I've seen. These prisons don't use lasers or shocks."

"Someone's coming." Karre pulled her arms out

from between the bars. She thrust her lock picking tool back into her upswept hair.

A new guard arrived, dressed similarly to the other men she'd seen. His nose had a crook across the bridge. "Only three new ones?"

"It's all they sent us," said the man who'd ordered the other two women away.

"How's it going, Edward?" Paige taunted, her face hardening to hide all emotion. Jayne watched in surprise, liking this version of Paige much better than the sulky one. "I see the nose is healing nicely."

"Lady Paige," Edward growled, glaring at her as if he wanted to pull the sword from his waist and run her through.

"Open the door, Eddie," Paige pouted her lower lip. "Let me break it again."

Edward grumbled, but didn't answer.

"I thought there were five new." Another of Edward's fellow barbarians joined them, completely ignoring Paige's comment.

"What's wrong, Brock? Don't I count anymore in your little ledger?" Paige asked.

"You are not new," Brock frowned. "Your lord is waiting for you and I do hope his punishment is harsh."

Paige's smirk wavered. Brock grinned.

"You already have one of these guys?" Karre whispered, grabbing Paige's arm.

"Two were not suitable. They were taken away," Edward answered Brock. His nostrils flared in distaste. "Too weak."

"Three will have to do," Brock said to Edward. As the two men walked off, he added, "I'll tell my Sera to make ready."

"Ladies," Paige whispered. "Welcome to Battlewar Castle."

LORD RONEN EYED his older brother as Lord Sorin lifted his arm toward the guard atop the castle wall, showing the bright red crest on his arm as he silently ordered the knight to lift the outer castle gate. The balding knight motioned down in understanding, disappearing over the side.

Like his brother, Ronen wore the red crest on his sleeve. The family symbol marked their respected ranks as leaders to two of the best armies in all of Staria. Very few would dare to challenge their word or honor.

Behind them, a small contingent of warriors rode in single file, followed by young valets and pages on foot. The boys led pack horses carrying the brothers' armor. It was a rare occasion that the warriors went without it.

Ronen rolled his shoulders. His simple, linen undertunic had been made from the naturally dark brown fibers of local plants. It fell loose and long over his tightly fitted black breeches with a long slit up the sides to ease the movements of the upper thighs. The warm day made an overtunic and cloak unnecessary. A woven belt wrapped loosely around his waist, holding a sheathed knife. Opposite the short blade, his sword hung from a shoulder scabbard that crossed his chest.

The steady clop of horses' hooves slowed while the oversized gate creaked its way up. The wooden crossbars were reinforced with iron and formed into giant spikes at the bottom. If the rope to the gate were cut as a man rode under, it would impale him and his horse under the deadly weight.

Everything about Battlewar Castle had been designed for war, just like all else in their land—from the long battlements that stretched around the main castle and Battlewar Town, to the secret passages and underground escape routes. This was the world Ronen had been born into. It was a world he knew well.

Yet, somehow, he always found it odd that on these occasions they rode not into the familiarity of battle, but to the only soft thing in a warrior's life. A woman.

Always before these ceremonies, something happened to his insides. As desperately as he wanted a woman to fill his bed and give him children, he was terrified that he'd actually find one. After what happened to Lord Sorin, Ronen wasn't in a hurry to find a mate.

"Relieve yourself beforehand. That was my mistake," Sorin said under his breath. It was the same advice he gave his younger brother each time they rode to the castle for a breeding ceremony. Since the loss of his first wife, Sorin's heart had been surrounded with bitterness. Well, loss was putting it lightly. The harlot Bianka had tried to seduce the whole of Firewall Castle before setting into motion the events that burned their ancestral home to the ground. When no one at Firewall would sate her, she ran away and threw herself at the enemy.

"There is no need to worry about me, Brother. I have better things to think of than binding myself to a woman," Ronen answered. A flurry of movement surrounded them as they rode into town. Women went about their work, busily preparing for the festival, ignoring the well-known sight of the warriors riding in. "At least coming here we'll get to feast on something other than dried meat and stale mead."

Intermingled with the peasants' homes in the outer bailey were a couple of barns, many workshops, small breweries and a large marketplace where the commoners sold their wares. Beyond the market, in the center of the city, a second, shorter wall encircled the inner bailey yard and castle. Contained within were the exercise yard where the knights trained, a small chapel, and the stables.

"Yea, there is that," Sorin agreed. Neither brother hurried to ride through town, instead occupying themselves with watching a group of children play. Five boys showed off for the attentions of a pretty girl. As one of the few female children, she'd be used to the notice. Even at a young age, the child would know how to manipulate the opposite sex to her whims. All females did.

Finally making it to the inner gate, Ronen sighed. A few of the soldiers glanced up, lifting their hands in greeting. The brothers nodded in unison, not needing to say another word as they solemnly made their way up the incline to the castle. It would all be over soon, and they'd be riding off to the battlefront at dawn.

2

JAYNE GLARED at the guard's back, hating him with every fiber of her being. All four women prisoners stood in the corridor outside the cell, but down the hall from the guards. Jayne found it odd that they didn't escort them properly, one in front and one in back, but it wasn't like they could run anywhere.

Jerking hard at her bound wrists, she ignored the burn of the rope against her skin. The longer she struggled, the tighter the binds became. She'd already put up a fight when they first tried to restrain her. Lilith and Karre made a proper show of struggling as they were tied, but Paige merely lifted her arms and let them work.

"The way I see it," Lilith said, "we don't have any choice but to join forces and pool our knowledge. I think we should gather intelligence. None of us seem to be from this world, so that means they had to get us all here somehow. If we keep our ears open, we'll find out how. There might be a way out of here yet."

"I've already looked for fairy rings when I was in the forest," Paige said. "I didn't even find evidence of fairies. Though, I'm not surprised. Fairies don't like wars and this place is nothing but one giant battlefield. I think my journey here was a one-way trip."

"Fairy rings?" Karre snorted with soft laughter.

"What?" Paige asked, looking around at the others. "Isn't that how you all got here?"

Jayne frowned. Fairies? Those things actually existed? She remembered vague tales of them from childhood. They were said to be horrible little creatures who, unlike Paige described, liked war, had supernatural powers and were to be avoided at all costs. If those mortal hellions were their only hope for escape, they were all in trouble.

"No more talking. They're ready for you," the guard announced, motioning his fist forward. "Let's go. March."

"BRING in the firsts so they may make their choice."

As the guard, Brock, made the announcement, Ronen looked up from where he'd been staring at the tips of his boots. A crescendo of laughter and cheering washed into the passageway from those gathered in the great hall to watch the ceremony. Being one of the six "firsts", it was Ronen's privilege to have first choice of the women awaiting them. He didn't plan on taking the honor.

"Any word from the front?" Ronen asked Sorin, who stood behind him in line. He fell into step behind a limping Sir Aidan, as they made their way forward. Behind Sorin, Sir Rian, Sir Vidar and Lord Serik awaited their chance to find a mate. Each man wore a different colored long tunic, reaching to the knees, over tight brown breeches. Woven belts wound their waists, the end straps hanging along the right thighs. "The scouts should have reported back by now."

"No, they must be delayed." Sorin kept his voice quiet.

"I have a man on the gate watching," Lord Serik put forth. "He's to notify me at once."

"I head for the battlefront near Spearhead as soon as this is finished," Sir Vidar said. "If any of you have messages..."

His words tapered off as they walked into the

main hall. A high table had been set with metal goblets and pitchers of mead and ale. Like the rest of the castle, the hall had been designed over centuries of careful planning and fine tuning. The large fireplace along a far wall radiated enough heat to warm the hall. The immensely thick stone insulated loud noises from the outside. Woven tapestries lined the walls in strips of material, showcasing coats-of-arms and important religious and political symbols.

Ronen first saw the other warriors, as they watched from the rows of tables spread out over the hall's floor. Some wore lightweight tunics, others leather jerkins like the guards, others light chainmail and pieces of armor, and still others wore no shirt at all. The effects of battle could be seen proudly displayed on their flesh—gruesome scars and tattoos of honor. Mixed in with the men were their women. Tight corset tops and flowing skirts had been designed to tease the Starian male's overactive senses.

When the Divinity otherworlders first approached them in the midst of battle, the Starians had almost slain the foreigners where they stood. They believed the oddly dressed creatures to be allies to the Caniba tribes. After much negotiation, investigation, a little bit of pleading by the Divinity scouts, and hours of council meetings, an alliance was formed with the otherworld beings. Divinity wished for samples of the blue mineral water, water that stayed warm no matter how long it sat away from another heat source. The blue water springs ran deep and wide, and there was no shortage of the mineral. Giving some away was a little enough consideration. In return, the Divinity leaders provided a resource much needed by the Starians—women.

As the firsts walked in, all gazes were focused in a single direction, toward the four women who'd been brought to Battlewar Castle's main hall. Out of the women Divinity sent, three were chosen as being of the right temperaments to stay. The new blood was just one of the reasons all the firsts were of high military rank or distinction.

Despite the fact that he'd relieved himself twice before coming down to banquet, Ronen found his body stirring with the thought of softer company. Denial wasn't easy for men as hot blooded as they were, and the mortality of war tended to make every second count.

His eyes turned to the women in curiosity. He hid a smile. The firelight shone through the white of their gowns, outlining their bodies in perfect temptation. He glanced over all of them, not really seeing their faces. His cock stirred, begging him to reconsider his decision. What was he fighting? A soft vessel in his bed? Someone to please his every decadent whim? A woman to service his member in any way he chose—sucking him, finishing him, offering every inch of herself to him? Ah, but to wake up in the morning and be able to go to the adjoining bedroom to have his morning arousal sucked out with soft, wet lips. To have a woman bathe him, using her hands to cleanse every inch of his body. Oh, the nights! To be able to bend her over and pound away in a tight, wet sheath. Ronen nearly came just thinking about it.

No. He had to stop thinking about sex. Ronen knew he had to stick with his decision. Like Sorin, he could stay strong. The men of Firewall would not take brides. Never.

"Mine."

What?

Ronen glanced around in surprise. The voice sounded like his brother's, booming over the hall. Surely, no. It couldn't be...

"Sorin?" Ronen whispered, glancing at the place next to him behind the table. His brother had stopped walking before reaching his seat.

"Mine," Sorin repeated.

Ronen couldn't believe his ears. He followed

Sorin's line of vision to the women. His brother ignored those in the stunned hall as he made his way to a pretty blonde with wide, frightened eyes. At least the woman wasn't a fool. With Sorin looming over her, she should be scared.

"Brother?" Ronen questioned, knowing the shock had to be evident in his voice. How could it be? That very day Sorin instructed him to stay strong and not fall for a woman's enchanting ways.

The skin at the back of his neck prickled. Someone watched him. Ronen glanced away from his brother only to find sinfully dark eyes studying him. His breath caught. Before when he'd looked at the women, he'd stared lustfully at their bodies. How could he have missed those bewitching eyes? That lush mouth parted in steady breath?

"You are mine." Sorin grabbed the blonde woman's ropes and held them tight, laying unmistakable claim.

Ronen barely noted the sounds of shock as murmurs ran over the crowd. His heart beat loud in his ears. Every nerve in his body shot with awareness. He'd seen women, but never had one struck him with such potent sexual awareness. Never had one made him want to throw her down, draw his tunic aside and begin wildly thrusting into her at the high table, not caring who watched.

What bewitching spell was this? He must fight it.

The herald made a weak noise, finally breaking the hushed tones of the crowd as he announced, "Rejoice, Lord Sorin has chosen!"

The statement came out more like a question than an announcement. Cheering erupted and still Ronen barely noted anything but the dark woman's steadfast gaze. She was tall and slender with flawless bronzed skin. Though she didn't move, he guessed she'd be graceful by the way she held her shoulders back and her neck long. She blinked, glancing to Sorin and the blonde before her gaze swept back to him.

Ronen smiled, hoping she'd return his lustful look. She didn't, but she didn't frown either. Commotion erupted and the woman turned her back to him to watch a fight in the crowd. It was as he suspected. She moved with poise and grace. This woman knew her body and how to use it.

"Come with me." Sorin ordered loudly, tugging his new wife behind him as he led the way from the main hall. He didn't even stay to feast with the others.

"Brother," Ronen insisted one last time, still not

believing his own eyes. The mighty Lord Sorin, his respected brother, had fallen. Again.

Women will be the death of us, Brother. You said so yourself.

"It is done, Ronen," Sorin answered before disappearing completely. "Tell Sera to send food to my chambers."

RONEN, hmm...

Jayne glanced between the two brothers, feeling sorry for poor Lilith. Lord Sorin was a giant amongst men, at least physically, and his ill humor left much to be desired. By the look on his face, it was quite possible Lilith was in for a beating. Feeling something akin to her days in the orphanage, a kind of helpless longing to join arms with her sisters and fight oppression, she took a deep breath. There was nothing she could do for Lilith. Childhood taught her that harsh lesson. The woman would have to survive whatever was coming to her and get past it. Jayne had her own problems.

She turned her attention forward. Sorin's brother seemed much more malleable. Plus, he already seemed to take an interest in her. The knight had stopped just short of drooling all over the hall floor as he looked at her chest.

Ronen. Easy target. Not at all hard like his brother.

Jayne had watched the firsts as they walked into the hall. The first one seemed too bitter and more interested in pointedly ignoring them. Sorin chose Lilith. Guess the man had a thing for blondes. Ronen's interest was obvious. By the way he eyed all the women's forms, he was just horny and looking for a place to find release. The fact annoyed her a little, but she assured herself she had no reason to care. Men got horny. It was the way of things. Besides, he meant nothing to her. Then there were the last three knights—two of whom seemed more interested in each other than the women and one who appeared disinterested in everything.

Ronen it is. Besides, handling one is better than taking on many.

Horny she could work with, perhaps even enjoy, especially when the man had the body of a warrior. Thick muscles held a tightly constructed frame, forming the perfect specimen of masculine beauty. But unlike the others, he had an ease to his movements. Dark waves framed his face, falling to his shoulders. He looked a lot like his brother, only shorter and less menacing. Then there were his eyes, dark and deep and expressive. She'd have to be careful of those eyes.

Jayne preferred to fight with her fists, but feminine wiles could work just as well. She let a small smile curl her lips. People around her talked, but she ignored them, focusing all her concentration on what she was doing. She kept her sights on her target. Ronen made a move to sit, but froze mid-action at her look.

That's right, sunbeam, I'm looking at you.

Stepping out of line, she walked right for him. Jayne let her hips sway, being sure to keep her back to the firelight. The action wasn't lost on Ronen. His eyes went straight to her waist.

Jayne felt the gaze of the crowd on her, but that didn't make her nervous. She was used to an audience. Still watching him, she stepped up the two stairs to reach the high table and lifted his goblet of liquor. With her hands bound, it was hard to hold on to the goblet, but she managed. Ronen practically fell into his chair. Closing her eyes, she drank deeply, purposefully letting little trails of liquid slide down her neck and into the ugly white gown's bodice. Jayne ignored the burning sensation that numbed her tongue and heated her throat and stomach.

When she finished, she set the goblet back down and licked her lips. Ronen's eyes followed the gesture, his mouth agape. Jayne put her bound hands on the table, leaned across the wooden top and stated, "Mine."

A round of gasps met her declaration. She was pretty sure by the look on Ronen's face that no woman had pulled this little stunt before. Well, they were sorely mistaken if they thought she was just going to stand there and be a timid little creature awaiting the first guy who decided he wanted to fuck her.

"Pardon me?" the man managed weakly, glancing back and forth as if he couldn't believe what he'd heard and needed outside confirmation.

She'd shocked him. Good. She would twirl his mind around in so many circles he wouldn't be able to see straight. By the time she was done with him, he'd try to conquer the entire country of Staria if she demanded it.

"Mine," she declared even louder.

He looked down at her chest before drawing his gaze back to her eyes. Ronen shook his head in denial. "It does not work—"

"Sunbeam, I'm sure it works just fine," she whispered, giving a meaningful glance down to his crotch.

Was she mistaken or was Mr. Happy poking his head up to play?

"What?" He looked at his lap, jumping a little. "Of course that works—"

Laughter broke out at the head table, cutting him off. His lips pressed tightly together.

Jayne pointed at the man who'd made Sorin's announcement. "Say it."

"My lady?" the man asked in surprise. Jayne rolled her eyes. Had none of these men ever seen a strong-willed woman before? "Lord Ronen, shall I...?"

"Say mine, Lord Ronen." Jayne leaned closer, parting her lips. Keeping her tone sultry and filled with erotic promise, she panted, "Say it. Say Jayne is mine."

She waited. His lips parted, as if he would answer but couldn't. He stared at her, stunned into obvious silence.

Without giving him warning as to her intentions, Jayne grabbed Ronen's face and jerked him to her. Her body fell across the tabletop and her elbows banged into the hard wood a little too firmly, but she ignored the little hints of pain. She'd expected the kiss to be a cold, calculated form of seduction. What she didn't expect was the rush of warm pleasure that started where their mouths met and ended in her toes. It was meant to be a quick, playful kiss, but it soon turned into more.

Jayne opened her mouth, sucking his bottom lip between hers. He tasted like liquor and something else she couldn't quite name. At first, he remained stunned, not kissing her back, but then his tongue slid into her mouth, rubbing and exploring. Their lips sawed together, rough and just a little awkward as they learned each other's rhythm.

Jayne gripped him tighter, becoming aware of her awkward position as she tried to hold onto his face for support. A utensil of some sort poked her ribs, digging in uncomfortably. The sound of cheering rushed over them, as the men from the lower tables went crazy with good-natured laughter and approval. Jayne was used to the crowds, to discomforts and pain. But she wasn't used to a mouth that tasted like his, or lips that felt so firm and good.

Her body tingled, each nerve ending seeming to fight for attention. But he didn't touch her, didn't grab her back, only returned the heated kiss she'd initiated. Well aware that her plan was quickly back-firing and she'd soon be lost to his touch and begging for things she didn't want to beg for, she pushed back. Breathing hard, she whispered to him, "Mine. Say mine. Say Jayne is mine."

"Mine," Ronen mouthed, as if entranced. He licked his lips slowly before he cleared his throat. Nodding, he repeated with more force so the cheering hall could hear, "Mine. Lady Jayne is mine."

"Good boy," Jayne blew him a quick kiss and stood, hoping she effectively put on a playful, unconcerned air. Inside, she still trembled. His taste was still on her tongue, teasing her with the promise of more.

Get control, Jayne, she ordered herself harshly. *It is time to perform. It is time to fight.*

Years of fighting in the ring and living as she did, trained her to quickly get all her emotions under control. He took her by surprise once with his taste, but now that she knew it, she would not let it happen again. Jayne turned to the announcer and arched a brow. Forcing a smile she didn't feel, she said, "Well? Get on with it."

"Rejoice!" the man called. "Lord Ronen has also chosen. The house of Firewall is complete. This is truly a day blessed by the gods!"

The hall broke out in a mixture of cheering and encouragement. Jayne winked at the crowd, waving audaciously to give them the performance they wanted. Just like her fans, none of these men really cared about her or the other brides. They wanted a show, something to gossip about later. And Jayne was always good at giving the crowd exactly what they paid for. Jayne suppressed a mocking laugh as she lowered her hand and turned to Ronen. *Poor, poor, Ronen. You're so out of your league.*

RONEN ENDEAVORED to slow his racing heart. Never in the history of his people had a woman stood up and announced her choice. But today, at this ceremony, it had happened to him. Lady Jayne chose to be his wife. She chose him. She wanted him. And she didn't hesitate, or doubt, or hold back. She sang her desire to the world, stroking his masculine pride for all to see, laying claim to him with her lips. Ah, those lips, so full, so pleasurable. Perhaps the gods knew he'd hesitate to say the words himself and gave her voice to initiate the claim. Either way, she belonged to him.

Ronen grinned. *Mine.*

The war gods smiled upon him for his deeds in battle and rewarded him with a gorgeous woman with an animalistic appetite to fuel his. He'd felt the envious eyes of the others as he whisked his new bride away to his chambers in the Mace Tower. None would dare to touch her, no matter how much they wanted to.

He breathed deeply, panting as if it had taken all his strength to walk the winding stairwell. Already he could envision tearing the clothes from her body, finding the soft womanly flesh, those secret crevices and gentle slopes only a lover could touch. He tried not to let his eagerness show, but he found himself slamming the door shut behind him.

"I hope this meets with my lady's approval." Ronen motioned around his tower room. None of the Starian men took pains to decorate their chambers and he was no different. A few necessary staples graced the room—a large bed with thick fur blankets, a weapons' wall to display and hold the majority of his belongings, the fireplace, a thickly cushioned chair and a trunk for the rest of his belongings. He motioned toward the far door next to his bed. "That door leads to your room."

"You live here?" she asked, her voice losing some of the smoky seduction of before.

"When I am here," he answered, wondering how long until she kissed him again. This time, she wouldn't stop. He wouldn't let her. "Normally I live at the battlefront or at Firewall Castle, my family home, before it burned to the ground."

"Firewall burned down?" Her mouth twisted slightly, and he wasn't sure he appreciated the humor she seemed to find at the irony.

He stiffened defensively. "It will be rebuilt when the resources can be spared."

Jayne's face sobered and she nodded, guarding her expression from him. Instantly, the playfulness came back, and he realized it was a practiced look, a defense, a way to hide her true emotions from the world around her. He wondered at it and opened his mouth to speak, but her words stopped him.

"This will do, I've stayed in worse." She made a show of walking around his room, touching his things with the delicate tips of her fingers. Each seductive brush sent an erotic shiver over his flesh, as if she marked all he was as her own. She ran her index finger over the long center indent of a sword. When she reached the end, she jerked her finger away, making a small noise of surprise. She stuck the digit between her lips and sucked. Ronen nearly came undone at the sight.

"Sharp," she whispered around her finger, indicating she'd cut herself.

Firelight caressed her every move, casting shadows in stark relief across her face. The orange glow caught up in her eyes, giving them a temptress's gleam. He swallowed over the hard lump in his throat. She didn't look away, and for the first time in Ronen's life he felt helpless.

"You have a lot of weapons." Jayne let the finger slip from her lips as she stepped brazenly toward him. Ronen couldn't move, could barely breathe. "Are they decoration or do you know how to use them?"

"Men must be..." His breathing deepened, and he could barely concentrate to answer as her eyes glanced to the bed and back again. It had been so long since he'd been with a woman. The camp followers were few and the number of men they serviced were many. "Must be prepared for battle."

"That doesn't answer my question, Lord Ronen. I asked if you knew how to wield your weapons." She smiled, an achingly seductive look. The white material of her gown clung to her breasts, teasing him as it hid her body from view. A strand of inky black hair fell over her smooth cheek. Every thought in his head centered on the hard heat of his cock. Never had it felt so full and thick, practically throbbing for attention.

41

Ronen nodded. "Yea, of course. I have held a sword since the night I was born and..."

Sanity left him. How could he think with her lips so close, so full and lush? How could he concentrate when every breath brought him the scent of a clean field, untouched by bloodshed? Never had a woman chosen him above all others. Sure, the camp followers enjoyed his bed on those rare moments he'd been in their company, but he was one of many to them. Lady Jayne chose him to be her one and the very idea of it spun his brain around in his head.

She touched the middle of his chest. It was just a gentle fingertip but enough to send a shiver over his entire frame. Jayne ran the caress down his tunic, just like she had with the sword blade. Reaching his waist, she stopped right next to his erection. "All your weapons?"

He tilted his jaw down in affirmation, realizing what she'd meant. Her hand cupped his cock, wrapping it tight through the material of his tunic and breeches. Ronen balled his hands into fists, curious to see what she'd do next.

"Yea," he managed, completely disarmed.

Jayne licked her lips and tugged at her gown. She pulled the material over her head, inching it up slowly. Strong, tan calves grew into perfect thighs.

Tradition dictated that she'd be naked under the gown, and he waited with bated breath to see the apex revealed. Naked, shaved flesh or soft black curls?

Absently, he tugged at the laces on his shoulder to loosen his tunic. The gown moved higher and his fingers stopped. Short curls formed into a strip to guard her sex, greeting him. Sleek muscles and rounded hips tapered to a flat stomach. With a deft swoop, she jerked the gown over her head. Breasts bobbed at the motion, a perfect handful. Dusky, round nipples puckered in the firelight, erect and begging for attention.

"Prove it," she ordered.

Ronen sprung into action, happy to obey. As he shoved his long tunic aside and tore at the laces to his breeches, she backed into the bed. He followed her, his pants falling over his boots to trap his feet. Jayne gasped, her eyes going to his full arousal.

No thoughts beyond the driving need to feel the warmth of her wet pussy passed through his mind. He needed her. He wanted her. He had to be inside her. Now.

Ronen pushed her shoulder and she landed on her back, her legs dangling over the side. The long strands of her hair spilled around her head, framing her gorgeous face. Her willingness was all the invitation he needed. Eagerly, he grabbed her legs, thrusting them open. Jayne's eyes widened in surprise. He wanted to take her then, hard and fast, but the bounce of her breasts caught his eyes. Leaning over, he buried his face between the soft mounds and groaned in pleasure. Her clean smell consumed him, scented by the distinct hint of her femininity.

He ran his hands over her sides, trying to explore everywhere at once. The urgency inside him wouldn't let him slow. Not yet. Not now.

Ronen pulled a taut nipple between his lips and sucked. She arched and moaned, grabbing his hair and tugging hard. The sound of her pleasure drove his aggressive lips on.

"Ah, in all the bloody battles of Staria," he cursed in frustration. His lips wanted more, but his cock refused to wait. The heat of her sex radiated onto his stomach. The call was too much for his libido to handle. Roughly, he grabbed her hips and dislodged his mouth from her breast. The wet nipple glistened, scorched with the orange firelight.

Ronen fumbled with his tunic, growling when he couldn't move the front of it fast enough. Mindless with passion, he brought himself to her sex. Jayne said something, but he couldn't hear her through the rushing sound of blood in his ears. The thick tip of his cock head slid along her moist heat, parting the curls. She felt so right, so slick and hot and ready.

He surged forward, pressing his cock into the velvet length of her sex. Ronen grunted, slowing in astonishment as the tight muscles of her pussy clamped down on him. Withdrawing, he worked his hips in easier thrusts, going deeper with each pass, not wanting to hurt her.

Jayne wrapped her legs around Ronen's waist, hooking her feet behind his ass. She forced him into her deep, making a strange noise as he penetrated her completely. His feet braced on the ground for leverage as he began to thrust. Her pussy clamped around him, giving the perfect amount of resistance.

Ronen felt like an untried youth, fumbling his way through his first time. A voice inside his head screamed at him to take his time, to enjoy the moment, but the desire raged and demanded satisfaction.

Jayne held onto his arm with one hand and rubbed her sex with the other. All the while, her legs controlled his movements. Ronen gripped the fur bedding, rocking wildly. He slammed into her, making her perfect breasts bounce. There was so much more he wanted to do to her. He tried to hold off, to stop the inevitable surge of release.

Muscles trembled and clamped down. He lost himself, spilling his seed with a hard jerk inside her body. His mouth opened wide and he groaned hoarsely. The loud sound echoed around them.

Jayne gulped for breath. As they had sex, her mind strayed from her purpose and she'd actually enjoyed herself. She refused to believe the fact meant anything, reasoning that it had been a very long time since she'd been with a man. And so what if she enjoyed it? Sex was meant to be pleasurable. It didn't mean she couldn't manipulate the man on top of her afterward.

"I would do that again and slower," Lord Ronen said, pushing up from her, "but I am expecting a report from the front lines."

What?

Jayne sat up in surprise.

"Your every comfort should be met next door. Look around and make it your own. If you've brought any personal items with you, they'll be delivered by the maids. A seamstress will come around. Please, direct her to make any gowns you'd like. I can well afford to clothe you." Ronen leaned over to grab his pants, pulling them up so he could re-lace them at his waist. His businesslike tone annoyed her.

What?! Where do you think you are going?

"But..." Jayne frowned, pushing up from the bed. Her first instinct was to cover her nakedness, but she refrained.

His eyes moved over her. "You wish for more? I will come back after my meeting to attend you."

"Wait, I think we need to talk." Jayne crossed in front of him, blocking his path to the door. This wasn't happening. *He* was dismissing *her*? Men did not dismiss her. She was Jayne Hart.

Ronen tilted his head. "I see nothing to discuss. If you have questions, the maids will help you find your way."

"I mean about this," Jayne waved around the room, "and us."

Did she just say that? Why in the world was she sounding all girly and clingy? What did she care if he didn't want to stay and cuddle in the aftermath? It's not as if they meant anything to each other.

"The choice was made." He tried to walk around her. Jayne again blocked him, forgetting her plan to manipulate him in her irritation. So what if she'd been planning on leaving him? His actions were unacceptable. "I see nothing to discuss. You are mine."

"Then I change my mind. There is no decision." Jayne put her hands on her hips, trying to rankle him. "I unchoose you."

Ronen's eyes narrowed in instant rage, the easy expression in his gaze fizzling out like water under fire. His shoulders tensed as he inhaled a deep, ragged breath. One very important fact became clear to her in that instant. Jayne underestimated the man before her. She'd seen him as the weakest of the pack, the one she could manipulate and push over. But she'd mistaken his easy manner for vulnerability. How could she have been so off in her assessment of her chosen opponent?

"You cannot change your mind," he growled, stalking her as she darted out of his way. "Law forbids it."

"I don't recognize your laws," she answered, just as loudly. Subtlety was not her strong suit and there was no point in searching for the trait now. With a forced laugh, she said, "I really don't recognize any dimension's laws."

"Tradition forbids it!"

"Curse your traditions. I don't recognize them either."

"*I* forbid it!" Ronen declared, his arms rising to the sides.

Jayne reacted on pure instinct, doing the only thing she knew to do. She drew back her hand and swung, saying more with her fist than she could with flustered words. How dare he treat her like property? Like some prisoner he could command? She was not some child to be locked away in an orphanage, kept like a dog to be beaten into obedience at the whim of her keepers.

Jayne had refused to think that there might be no escape until that moment, when his eyes flashed and his voice lifted. She didn't like being helpless. Plan one seduction-manipulation had been a complete failure.

Then it is time for a new plan. I'll go with what I know best.

Shock filtered over his expression for a millisecond before contact. Ronen didn't try to stop her as fist met flesh. His head snapped back, but he didn't stumble. Jayne leapt onto the bed, expecting him to make a fight of it. Once she subdued him, if she subdued him, she'd make a run for it. Giant prairies and Paige's monster-filled forest wouldn't stop her from trying to escape. Even if she had to live in the dirt for the rest of her days, she'd do it on her own terms. Free.

As she reached for a knife on his wall, his soft words stopped her. "You signed your deal. You cannot escape it and neither can I. We are together in this."

Wondering at the way he phrased his words, she turned. Already his eyes swelled with the red of her hit. Why wasn't he fighting back? She knew the punch had to hurt. The bioengineered, metal "boxing gloves" Divinity had grafted beneath her skin would see to that. He should have been raging in anger at her attack. Jayne's hand again automatically started to reach for the wall of weapons, but halted midair, unsure how to proceed. Why wasn't he fighting?

"Perhaps you should stay here in the room while your temper cools." Ronen grabbed her white gown from the floor and left, gripping it tight in his palm. As the door shut with a decisive thud, she stared after him in confusion.

"I've really underestimated you, Lord Ronen." Jayne bit her lip thoughtfully. Instead of grabbing a weapon, she went to look inside the room he said was for her. The furnishings were nice, if a person was into the domestic scene. Dark wood, simply carved, made up the furniture. The bed looked to be the same size as Ronen's, with white fur on the coverlet instead of gray. Jayne would never sleep in such a fluffy concoction. A dressing table arranged with little colorful bottles stretched along one wall next to a circular inlet with tiny slit windows and an oversized chair. The only way in or out was through Ronen's chamber.

Having no desire to go inside and explore, she shut the door. Air stirred around her naked body. If he thought stealing her clothes was going to keep her locked in her tower, then he'd sorely misjudged her. Striding to the trunk at the end of his bed, she flipped it open and began to dig.

How dare he walk out on me!

3

"THESE FOREIGN WOMEN have bewitching powers. We should never have entered into an agreement with the otherworlders."

Ronen listened to his brother's bitter tone and nodded in agreement. Sorin fared little better in his choice of mate, already regretting his hasty actions as he glared at those gathered in the hall. Tension rolled from the lord's shoulders and Ronen knew better than to ask for details. When Sorin was angry, it was best to leave him be. One irritating move and he'd rip a man's head from his body. But, for all that rage, he would never lay a rough hand on his new bride. Even with Bianka, he'd never struck her and that woman deserved it.

Ronen related to the feeling and practically growled at the shadowy reflection in his pale yellow drink. His desire had been sated, somewhat, and replaced by fury. She tried to get out of their arrangement. How dare Jayne choose him, kiss him like that in front of everyone at the breeding ceremony and then try to leave him. This was his life, not a game. His stomach tightened into big knots. Only one thing had changed from her decision to take him as a mate. They'd had sex. By the teeth of the damned, it had been awhile. Had he truly been such a bad, clumsy lover? The idea that he'd failed kept him from repeating the act a second time, no matter how enthusiastically his cock wished for him to run back up the Mace Tower stairs. He needed to calm the lust running rampant in his blood so he could concentrate and do it right.

"Witches," Ronen muttered, waving to a maid to refill his goblet. As the woman dared to make her way to the ill-tempered brothers, Sorin motioned Sir Rian to join them at the table. By the un-tortured look of his expression, Ronen assumed the man hadn't chosen a woman.

Lucky knight. Would that we had been so smart.

"Any word from Lord Serik's man? Do the

Caniba armies march against the forces at Spearhead?" Sorin asked.

"They do not march yet, but Lord Martin suspects it will be soon." Rian took a seat next to Sorin, his steady brown gaze meeting both men briefly. "Sorceress Magda's scouts were captured in the southern marshes, but at the loss of two good men —Richard of Daggerpoint and Peeter of Fallenrock. They died well and were not taken by those cannibals. Sir Vidar goes to lead the interrogations. He has already left with his new bride."

"Vidar, too?" Ronen let loose a long breath. It would seem all three of the foreign women had been claimed, not that it surprised him. Women were scarce and men were lonely. The fourth, Lady Paige, had been an arguably spiteful gift from the fairies and would go home with her husband, Sir Aidan, to be punished as he saw fit. Perhaps the foreign women were defective and should be sent back to their worlds. Surely Divinity only gave away those they needed to be rid of. The Starians should have known the deal was too sweet an offer. Blue mineral water for willing wives? More like water for witches.

"Yea, Vidar, as well." Rian agreed. "Though he looked about as pleased as the two of..." The words tapered off and Rian gave the brothers a sheepish look.

"And Aidan?" Sorin asked.

"He did not look well when he left Battlewar." Rian sighed, leaning forward to grab an abandoned goblet at the head table and lift it to a maid. She nodded, running to fetch him a clean one. "Nor did Lady Paige."

"This is a bad year for finding mates," Ronen put forth grimly. "Perhaps we should cancel the ceremonies, especially those involving the otherworlders."

"The decisions are made," Sorin broke in, giving Ronen a look of warning. He would not like any hint of dishonorable thoughts, especially not in front of witnesses. As the oldest brother, he took their familial duty very seriously. "There is no reason to contemplate them."

Rian nodded once in agreement. "Though, it does not mean we have to choose the women they send."

"What other news?" Ronen inquired.

"Not much else. Lines hold strong on both sides. Vidar hopes to discover where the Sorceress's encampment lies. We suspect she is in the Hanging Forest, but we can't find any who will speak of her.

All they say is she lives in the ground like a serpent, rising up from the earth to feed. It's impossible to tell her numbers, and Sir Fredrick is still not the same since being held her prisoner. We must leave him in a room lined with mattresses to keep him from bashing his own skull against the stone walls of his chambers. He must eat without trencher or knife and a guard watches him at all times." Rian didn't reveal anything they didn't already know, more or less, and the news of Fredrick saddened Ronen's heart.

One of the self-proclaimed queens of the Caniba tribes, Sorceress Magda was as elusive as she was cruel. It was whispered that she studied the black arts and her followers, before being allowed to bear the mark of her soldiers, were made to dance with the serpent. Whoever endured the serpent's poison and lived was allowed to serve and they did so with blind obedience and obsession. Over the last four years, she'd been one of the more aggressive Caniba factions attacking the borders.

"We should ride to the borderlands," Ronen said, lightly touching his bruised eye. He'd had worse injuries in battle, but somehow this one stung more. "We will be of more use there."

"We have not been summoned," Sorin lowered his voice to a whisper, "and, unless the king orders otherwise, we will be forced to bring the women with us."

"Not if they become with child," Ronen reasoned, suddenly sorry he'd spoken the idea out loud. He wanted children, many of them, but he was certain the woman abovestairs wouldn't be so inclined.

Sorin tensed, a severe frown crossing his features. "We would do better to pray for war, Brother."

"Witches," Ronen grumbled, falling into the comfort of his foul mood. "The gods have cursed us with witches."

"Yea, these be a poor lot of women," a brunette maid grouched as she lifted her arms over her head to hang a fresh tapestry in the long corridor. Jayne stayed crouched beside a door inset into the stone, shaded from their view. A large metal urn on the floor reflected the blurry figures just enough that Jayne could watch what they were doing.

"What do you expect, Nan? I told you foreigners wouldn't suit our men as well as we." A second servant laughed with pride. Her thick red hair was piled high on her head. "Only Starian women know how to properly please Starian men."

"It's too bad Lord Sorin and Lord Ronen didn't take their two south like the others," Nan said. "I wonder if Ronen's wench is anything like Lady Lilith."

"That one thinks she's the Princess of the Black Tower, or my name isn't Hannah. Barely said a word to us while we were up there. Princess Lilith, that one. Well, I will show her princess." Hannah lifted her foot and pretended to kick.

"Barely did a thing to poor Lord Sorin," Nan giggled. "Did you see the poor knight walking funny like his serpent was still full of venom? How hard is it to lie back and let a man have his way? I daresay I looked forward to an ease in that nobleman's temper. Now she's gone and made him worse. He practically strangled Sera in the stairwell. She was lucky those stairs are so close to the kitchen so we would have been able to hear her screams."

Hannah gave a dark laugh, stepping back to eye the tapestry on the wall. She nodded once in approval of it. "Don't you worry about that. I took her clothes out with the old bedding. One look at her naked body, even one as skinny as hers, and Lord

Sorin will take what he needs from her, willing or no. That will cool his beast."

"Should we check on Ronen's wench?" Nan asked, as the women walked away.

"He's drinking with his brother and did not order us up to his tower. Let his wench fend for herself. If his dark mood is any sign, she knows nothing of spreading her legs either." Hannah laughed, prompting Nan to join her. They lifted up the rolled tapestry they'd just replaced and carted it off down the hall under their arms. "In some ways it serves the lords right for choosing otherworlders from the Divinity deal. It's not what the gods intended for our people. Had they been patient and waited for a blessing, they'd have been given a woman who knows how to move her hips."

Like you're some prize to have in bed, miserable cat. Jayne frowned after the women, as she pushed to her feet. *I know how to please a man. Lord Ronen wasn't complaining when I got done with him.*

Thinking of how desperate Ronen had been only made her eager to turn around and return to his bed. The fear of being trapped stopped her. She could not stay here and be some man's love slave—even if the mere thought of him caused her legs to tremble. The fact that she wanted him made her fear him all the more. Thankfully, in such a world as this, the man would never come to care for her. He probably wouldn't even bother searching for her should she run. Or, if he did, he'd soon give up.

Since Ronen confiscated her gown, she simply took one of his tunics—a long black affair with a red patch on the chest. The sleeves were too long so she cut them off to uncover her hands. Then she used one of the strips to tie her hair back away from her face and the other to sheathe the blade she had tied to her upper thigh with a piece of belt. The decorative jewel hilt of the knife would make for good barter should she have a need to trade it. The short boots she'd stolen from a laundry room pinched her toes but were better suited to running through a prairie than bare feet.

She resisted the urge to follow after the servants to give them a piece of her mind. Then again, she could always thank them for their gossiping help. With Karre and Paige out of the castle, it would mean she only had to find Lilith. Sure, she didn't really owe the woman anything and, by all reasoning, she could have left Lilith to fend for herself, but Jayne wasn't like that. When a child slipped through the orphanage's bars, they helped all they could through behind them. Besides, she didn't want to go it alone. Regardless of her strength and bravery, this was still a strange land and a strange people. Jayne could use all the friends she could get. Nothing made faster friends than two people fighting for the same cause—freedom.

Already she'd made slow progress through the castle. It would seem most of the occupants were in the main hall drinking in celebration, so she stuck to the narrow passageways and mazelike tunnels that wound around the central room. The blue-gray stone walls and minimal decorations made it hard to navigate—especially if the maids continued to change the tapestries.

Jayne had run into more than a few amorous couples in the act of "taking the venom out of the serpent". One pair, a knight and his busty mistress, went at it on a stairway leading down to utter darkness. Their clothes were simply pushed aside while they fucked hard and desperate, grunting like wild beasts. Another man found pleasure by his mistress's lips as she busied herself beneath the front flap of his long tunic. He kept his eyes closed, moaning softly as the shape of her head bobbed up and down beneath the green material.

By far the most salacious was the servant who took two men at once, sandwiched between them as one pressed his back into the wall. Jayne saw them through a cracked door, perfectly positioned as if they invited others to watch what they did. When she crawled past, she noticed that was exactly what was happening. A third man sat on a chair, stroking himself as he enjoyed the sexual exploits of the performers.

Jayne had been to wild parties before, but never on such a grand scale as this. There were more couples locked in various ways and not a one noticed her as she passed. Maybe this castle was a brothel of some sort and these soldiers were here on leave from their home dimension. Is that what happened? They paid the castle Madame to claim a woman in some strange custom in the front hall, took their fill of them and then left the woman for the next man? Did they know who she was? Was getting a chance to fuck the famous Jayne "The Sweet" Hart some sort of high-dollar draw? Rich men had offered her a lot of money in the past—not that she'd ever taken it. She'd seen women on the street who fell into such a life for the sake of survival. Jayne was surviving on her own. She didn't need to be a man's paid whore. But, with losing so much money in the last fight for Divinity, had they come up with a way for her to pay them back? She wondered how much Ronen paid for her. Was that why he hesitated when she lay claim? The whore wasn't supposed to pick her patron? Or had he been calculating the worth of her cost? Is that why he got mad? He'd paid for her and she was trying to renege on a deal she hadn't realized she'd made?

I'm going to throw up.

"All the more reason to find Lilith and get out of here," she said under her breath. Never having played the part of the prude, Jayne didn't relish the idea of being any man's permanent or temporary plaything. If luck were on her side, she'd find that kitchen and the Black Tower steps soon.

She hurried down several corridors, doing her best to navigate through the halls unseen. Slowing as she neared a sharp corner, she listened first and peeked second. The faint sound of padded footsteps caught her attention before being drowned out by a boisterous laughter from the main hall. She'd traveled along the back wall of the main hall, ending up on the opposite end of the castle. Jayne tensed, inching back, her legs ready to make a run for it should a boisterous knight happen upon her.

A woman appeared, dressed in a black tunic similar to the one Jayne now wore, only the sleeves were rolled instead of cut, and the lady had wrapped a belt around her midsection. Seeing the long, straight blonde hair, Jayne nearly laughed with relief. Lilith. It would seem luck did favor her. She suppressed the urge to make a sound and bit her lip.

Lilith appeared to be alone, as she glanced first at the noisy hall and then back the other direction. With no way to call out to her for fear of drawing attention, Jayne crept up behind her and slid her hand over the woman's mouth.

"Hey," Jayne whispered in her ear, pulling her back past the stairwell she'd emerged from into a hidden inlet.

Lilith tensed, jerking in alarm at the sudden attack. She began to claw at the hand over her mouth, but Jayne turned her around so they faced each other. Lilith instantly relaxed, though her eyes remained wary.

Pressing close in the tight space of the narrow alcove, Jayne glanced down meaningfully and gave a light laugh. "Looks like we shop at the same store."

Lilith followed Jayne's gaze downward, but didn't answer.

"I overheard the maids talking. I was about to come up to the tower to get you." She looked at Lilith's bare feet. "Couldn't find any shoes to steal? Follow me, there's a laundry room this way. They have shoes."

Still Lilith didn't answer. The poor thing looked terrified and completely out of her element. She almost felt sorry for those wide blue eyes. What had that giant of a man Lord Sorin done to her? Surely, he didn't break her spirit already? The maid said nothing happened between Lilith and Sorin, but seeing the woman's pale face, Jayne wasn't so sure. Some men had strange tastes.

Deciding scared company was better than none, she hoped to spur the woman into action and put her at ease. Jayne leaned forward and kept her voice low. She tugged on Lilith's arm. "Come with me. I promise Lord Sorin won't touch you again, but you have to make a fight of it."

"Wait." Lilith refused to move.

Damn those almost innocent blue eyes. They instantly drummed up protective, big-sister feelings inside of her. She'd seen that look on the faces of children as they came to the orphanage—scared, confused, hopeful and still capable of love. And then the years would hit them and Jayne would watch those eyes fade and the hope die. The death of the soul was worse than physical death and hurt a lot more.

"What did they do to you?" Lilith whispered, as if scared to hear the answer. "Did they hurt you?"

Jayne tried not to think about how great Ronen's body felt inside hers and lied, "No, they didn't touch me, but I don't want to give them the chance to."

How could she admit to what she'd done? Especially if someone had gotten paid for her to do it?

"What are you planning to do?" Lilith asked with a tinge of desperation.

"Karre and Paige have been taken south by a couple of the barbarians. With any luck, we'll be able to find them. Paige seems to know her way around this backwater place." Jayne again tried to pull her. "The timing is perfect. They're in there having a party and getting drunk. It will be dark soon. We'll find a way out of the castle and wait until nightfall. If we travel by dark, we should make it through the prairie to the forest. From there, by the grace of some miracle, we'll find a trail to follow—"

"You're going to escape?" Lilith jerked Jayne back, keeping her from leaving. "You can't, Jayne. I've talked to a few of the servants. If we displease them, I think they might kill us."

"They didn't kill Paige for running," Jayne reasoned.

"Yet," Lilith asserted. "How do you know that's not what they're taking her south for? You heard the guard. Her master might delve out a harsh punishment."

Jayne felt the color draining from her face. "What would you have us do? We can't stay here forever, waiting for them to get tired of us. What if they try to philter us like the others—whatever that means. What if they make us take on more men? If you saw what I saw walking these hallways, you'd know we have to run. I can't stay here and be a whore and that's exactly what I think this place is. A whorehouse."

"I was told the philter is a drug to make you forget you've been here. They said those women from the cell with us were sent home because they were unsuitable."

"I don't think that'll work for us. We've been chosen to stay," Jayne drawled mockingly. Though, it did sting that those whiny bitches from the cell got to go home and they were stuck here. Maybe she should learn to cry and pout more. Perhaps then Ronen would ship her off to be rid of her. Jayne wondered if she even had it in her to muster up fake tears. Fists were much more her thing.

"I think we should stay in the castle for now. Sorin didn't seem too keen on passing me around to all the men." Lilith reached to touch her shoulder lightly. "Are you sure you weren't hurt? Did your man...? Did he make you...?"

"Ronen? No. He didn't try to pass me out." Jayne said, only to add silently, *yet*. "I would have ripped off his balls had he tried."

Lilith's eyebrows lowered in thought as she reasoned, "I can learn more here in civilization than in the woods. If we keep our heads low and try to behave, maybe we'll find a way home. I think we'll have better luck here at a castle than in the wild. Besides, running is too big of a gamble. How will we survive in the wilderness? How will we eat? What kind of animals are in the forest? Poisons? Flora and fauna? Insects? What about the people the Starians are fighting? What's out there could be much, much worse than what is in here. Paige seemed really scared when she spoke of the monsters."

"Paige could be lying. This castle could be a theme place and beyond the compound is a thriving society with technological advances. Whatever it is, I can't stay here. I'm not scared of dying," Jayne put forth grimly. "But I will never live as some man's slave. Please come with me."

Jayne followed Lilith's contemplative gaze as she looked to the main hall. They heard a low murmur of conversation with the random bouts of laughter filtering in. If they were going to leave, they needed to go now while the men were distracted with their party. Maids or knights could happen upon them at any moment.

"I can't go with you," Lilith decided. "I'm taking my chances here."

"Do you have a plan?"

Lilith nodded, not looking too sure of herself. "I think so. If I find a way to escape, I'll do my best to let you know about it."

"And if I do, I'll try to send word," Jayne glanced down and smiled, "in a pair of shoes."

"Good luck to you then." Lilith looked as if she might hug her, but stopped and instead held out her hand.

"And to you." Jayne clasped it briefly. "Don't let them break you. One way or another, we're going home. I promise."

"She is my wife." Ronen stumbled into the wall and frowned at the stone. How did that get so close? He pushed away, continuing up the Mace Tower stairwell, only to hit the other side. When did the stairwell become so narrow? "I will grab her, shake her and tell her, 'you are my wife, my lady, um, my Lady Jayne'."

It was a plan. A great plan. A brilliant plan. She'd have to listen to his decree. He was a lord after all and a great leader. Men had to listen to him, why not his bride?

"Ugh," Ronen grabbed his head as his vision swam. He would declare his position and then to bed. Tomorrow he'd talk to Sera about the mead. It should not have been so strong. He'd only had...

Ronen frowned. How much did he drink? He started to sit down on the stairs only to catch himself. Why didn't Sera insist he eat something? Or had she? He vaguely remembered throwing a tray of food onto the hall floor.

"Jayne." He'd forgotten in all his irritation to order food sent to their room for her. Hopefully, Sera remembered. The servant was usually good about those things. It's why she held the position of honor in Battlewar Castle. "Jayne will be rested and fed, and now it will be time for her to listen as I explain her role as my wife. Starting with my bed."

The thought quickened his steps as he hurried the rest of the way to his chambers. Desire heated his liquored blood, causing his skin to tingle and his cock to lift high and proud. He opened the door, his eyes eagerly seeking the bed. She wasn't there. Then again, why would she be? This was not her room. Crossing over the floor with purpose, he opened the door to where she would be sleeping.

"Jayne," he announced, pointing his finger into the darkness. "You are my wife and that means something."

She didn't answer. The fireplace in her room had not been lit so he couldn't see beyond the soft glow coming from his own chamber.

"Jayne," he continued, holding onto the door frame. "You are a Lady of Firewall and there will be no more talk of you leaving me. The decision is made. I understand that there is nothing in the tradition of warriors choosing women from a group they just met that ensures a great, great, ah..." He frowned, blinking hard. "A great joining of two households, er, people. What I mean to say is at least I didn't raid your village like my ancestors used to do, grab you and cart you off to my bed. And you chose me for a husband without having ever met me. That must mean something. I didn't ask for a wife, didn't pray to the gods for one. You just happened."

Still she said nothing. It was just as well she listened. He had much he wanted to get straight with her.

"Though, many of us agree the raids were easier. That way we did not have to leave the battlefront to bother with a ceremony so far north in the kingdom." He paused, shaking his head. What was he talking about? Oh, his wife. "You are my wife and the gods chose you for me as a reward to my great service in battle. They brought you from your otherworld and we will have sons and if so blessed daughters when I am not at war. I will take care of you and protect you."

Still nothing.

"I realize earlier I might have been overeager, but I should like to make that up now." Desire at the idea of bedding her curled within him, stirring his lust to settle heavy in the already thick mass of his cock. "We Starian men have needs and I would not have you turning me away from your bed, but, if you command it, I will leave you be. I am not a monster."

She didn't answer. Did that mean she accepted him? He took a step toward where the bed would be hidden in the darkness. Reaching out, his fingers bumped into the mattress. Excitement pumped in his veins and he prayed to all his gods that he'd be able to satisfy her this time. His hands remembered the feel of her skin. His mind conjured the silk of her flesh, the softness of her breasts, the athletic perfection of her form.

Pulling out of his tunic, he tossed it aside. Ronen crawled onto the bed, feeling around for her. Whispering, his hands shook, as he admitted, "I would have happiness between us, Jayne, and perhaps, in time, affection. I know it's not required in a marriage, or even sought, but I would have us come to care for each other."

Why wouldn't she speak? He'd laid bare his soul, a feat harder than facing a hundred Caniba warriors in battle.

"Jayne?" His hand slid over the bed. The coverlet hadn't been ruffled. In disbelief, he kept searching. If she wasn't in here and she wasn't in his chambers, then...

The realization sobered him greatly. She wasn't there. He leapt from her bed. Running to his room, he grabbed an unlit torch and thrust it into the fire. Once lit, he went back to search for her. Torchlight cast over her unruffled bed and revealed the unused chair and vanity.

"Jayne?" he called, knowing he wouldn't receive an answer from the empty space. He checked his own room again, his gaze scanning over the bed and trunk. Finally, they landed on this weapons' wall to the spot where the jeweled blade he'd had since childhood should have been.

Ronen's first thought was the Caniba had snuck in and stolen her away. He quickly dismissed it. That was not how the Caniba fought. They attacked in the open, crazed man-eating beasts without reason or thought, driven by their primal needs. There was no way they'd slip through the gates, pass through town and a castle filled with knights and servants. Not looking and acting as they did—smelly, pelt-covered monsters with sunken eyes and sharpened teeth.

But if not their enemies, then it would mean she'd left him on her own. Hoping that she'd gone in search of food, or to explore, he rushed down the stairs still carrying his torch. He turned away from the main hall's entrance, going to the maze of halls running behind it. Seeing a servant, he handed her the torch. "Have you seen Lady Jayne?" At the woman's blank look, he clarified, "My wife. Have you seen her?"

The maid shook her head in denial. "No, my lord."

Ronen's heart beat heavily in his chest, echoing in the caverns of his ears. With each person who told him they hadn't seen her, the more panicked he became. The servants and guards joined in the search, spreading from inside the castle to the inner bailey.

Sera brought him herbs to help clear his head of the liquor, but clarity of thought only convinced him that Jayne had run away. Thoughts of his brother's first wife, Bianka, filled him with fear. What if he was cursed to relive Sorin's pain? Seeing the torture the evil woman had put Sorin through had torn at Ronen's heart. His brother had never been the same. A vital part of him had died, leaving a hard shell.

What if Jayne did to him what Bianka had done? What if she suffered the same fate?

In the very short time he'd been in her presence, Ronen didn't suspect the lady to be a selfish witch who drained the very life force from those around her. But then, Sorin had thought Bianka a tender heart in need of protection. Only later did her true, cruel nature come out. Her own people had shoved her into a fairy ring to be rid of her.

Ronen thought of what he'd been prepared to confess to his new bride, of his desire for something more, deeper, in their lives together. If the men were to find out it would be an embarrassment, let alone if word reached his older brother. How could he have been so stupid? How could he have bared his soul like that? It was a small blessing she hadn't heard, and he would not be making the same mistake twice.

"Ronen!" Sorin stormed across the torch lit bailey. Tension radiated from his stiff movements and he looked like he'd crawled through the very heart of Caniba. "What news is this?"

"Jayne is gone." Ronen took a deep breath, trying to hide the pain he felt at admitting the words out loud. "You were right. I should have stayed strong and not allowed her to influence my choice. Now I have dishonored—"

"No," Sorin stated, cutting him off. He put his hand on Ronen's shoulder, drawing him near as he quietly stated, "We will find her before she dishonors you or our family. Are any horses missing?"

"No." Ronen shook his head.

"Then she is on foot. With the celebration tonight it would have been easy for her to slip through town and out the gate without being noticed. None of us thought another bride would run from her wedding night so soon after Lady Paige. It will not happen a third time. Precautions will be made in the future." Sorin motioned his hand to a nearby page. "Our horses!"

Several of the men heard the command and

hurried to order their mounts as well, without having to be asked to ride out.

"We will find her, Brother," Sorin assured him. "Feet cannot outrun horses, even if she has hours upon us. And, if you have to, you will lock her away in a tower to keep her safe. This will be made right."

Ronen didn't answer. He knew Sorin also thought of Bianka's escape. Only, with Bianka, they'd not found her in time. Firewall Castle had been closer to the borderlands and all who lived there were busy with the fire. By the time Sorin and Ronen were told of her disappearance, it was too late. She'd crossed over the Caniba border and propositioned one of their raiding parties. First, they took what she offered, then they took her valuables and her horses, and then they took her for food. It was a nightmarish day they would never forget.

"She is not Bianka," Sorin hissed, willing it to be so with the hard tone of his voice. Even so, his gaze wavered in its certainty. Turning, he yelled, "Twenty men. We ride!"

Ronen blinked, spurred into action as he strode to take his horse. Two pages arrived, carrying weapons from the armory for the brothers. Another handed Ronen a tunic shirt.

By all the bloody battlefields, do not let the Caniba take her.

"Good ride, my lords!" the young boys yelled, unable to hide their excitement. How little they understood what happened.

Ronen ignored them, grabbing the reins and swinging up before slipping on his shirt. Then, taking the weapons, he rode for the gate, letting the horse guide the way as he tightened the cross strap of the scabbard over his shoulder and across his chest to his waist. To himself, he cursed, trying to forget his fears as he held onto his anger. "My wife has run away. The gods truly frown upon me."

4

As they rode through town, word spread about the missing bride and, with the peasants searching to find Jayne, she wouldn't be able to hide within the city walls. Ronen ordered six of the men to ride north to investigate the only trail leading away from Battlewar Castle. The treacherous route was an unlikely escape, but he would not leave ground uncovered. The underground tunnels and secret passages were locked away and too hard to get to without knowledge of the castle.

Ronen didn't speak as he led the remaining knights in the most logical direction—south to the Hanging Forest. The full moon shone bright over the prairie grasses, giving the knights enough to see by as they rode hard over the fields. So many people had passed that way over the years it was hard to distinguish fresh tracks in the night.

Sorin rode next to him, equally as quiet. He gripped his reins, forcing the animal faster as if he couldn't run from the castle fast enough. Ronen knew his brother well and could easily gather he ran from Lady Lilith. As head of the family, Sorin would be duty bound to capture the wayward Jayne, but he didn't have to look so inclined to do it.

The wind hit him hard, causing his hair to slap across his face. All the knights riding with them had trained at Battlewar as children. They knew the prairie and the forest. They would find her.

I will find her.

"She could not have gotten far on foot," Sorin yelled over the noisy wind. The horses naturally slowed as they neared the tree line. If they rode too fast, the horses could lose their footing and break a leg. "No matter how much Divinity told them, these women cannot know what lies in our forests. With luck a bird will frighten her and we'll find her soon enough."

The words were hardly comforting. There was more to the forest than birds and innocuous insects. Wolves, wild boar, bucks, any number of creatures could attack her. He touched his sore eye. Though she threw a decent punch, he doubted she'd survive a pack of hungry wolves. What if he couldn't get to her before something bad happened?

Sorin lifted his hand and pointed to the east then west, ordering the knights to spread out over the distance and begin their search. Each man would remain within whistling distance, should the lady be found. When he finished, Ronen finally answered, "She does not know what she faces, even with my knife to arm her."

"The forest at night can be a daunting thing," Sorin comforted. "Rest assured in that we are far away from the battlefront. The Caniba tribes will not have ventured this far. One look at a wild beast and she'll scream for us to save her."

"Let's ride," Ronen urged his horse left, away from his brother. Pulling his sword, he gripped it tight, feeling some comfort in the weapon's weight.

By all the blood-soaked fields of my ancestors, when I find you, lady wife, I will follow Sorin's advice to lock you away where you will be safe.

In less than a day his life had changed drastically. It hardly seemed real. Maybe she had bewitched him or used a poisoned fragrance brought from her alien world. Whatever the cause, duty demanded he find

her and honor their joining—whether she wanted to
or not.

X

JAYNE REFUSED TO STOP RUNNING. The burn in
her thighs was nothing new and actually comforted
her in its familiarity. Physical exertion she could
handle, even if the path was rocky to nonexistent,
littered with forest trash and blocked by dense trees.
She tried to stay in the moonlight, avoiding the
darkest part of the forest, using a stick to swipe spider
webs out of her way. The more distance she put
between herself and the castle, the less chance she'd
have of being found. Of course, Lord Ronen might
not even look for her. Why should he? They technically just met.

Maybe she could negotiate a portal jump with
the Caniba "monsters". In fights, there were always
two sides and Jayne knew nothing about the Starian
enemy. The Caniba might be a technologically
advanced race whose use of electricity made the
Starian people think of them as witches. Such super-
stitious nonsense wasn't unheard of.

She hated having so many theories in her head,

not knowing which were real. Brothel dimension? Otherworld filled with beasts? A role-playing plane?

Suddenly, she stopped, gasping for air as she came face-to-face with a sharp cliff of dirt. The forest had shifted long ago, leaving a precipice filled with random plant shoots and a strange pink-tinted moss. Feeling along the darkened wall, she dug her fingers into the dirt. It crumbled, tumbling down to her feet. Though unsteady, she grabbed the knife and began to scoop out small footholds in the cliff. It wasn't so high she couldn't manage to climb up.

She breathed hard, the harsh sound drowning out the quiet chirps of insects singing in the forest. Jayne tried not to think about the isolation, putting the uneasy fear from her mind. It was for the best. Lilith would have slowed her down.

Jayne was used to being alone, but alone with other people. In the orphanage she'd slept in a room filled with other children—probably the closest thing to a family she'd ever had and she never talked to any of them anymore. After she ran away, it was a city filled with other homeless. Then, when Coach Wagner caught her fighting one of his students for pocket change, she'd lived in the boxer dorms. From there, she entered Divinity's entertainment circuit.

Never really connected to the masses around her, but surrounded all the same.

"Don't think of the past," she whispered, trying to urge her tiring body on. She pulled the longer pieces of the stolen tunic shirt through her legs and fastened them into short pants with her belt and sheathed the knife at the back of her waist. "Concentrate on the now. Come on, Jayne, let's do this. Climb the wall."

Jayne took a deep breath and held it, thrusting her foot into a carved step before launching her body up the side. Silence surrounded her. The insects had quieted. She ignored the stab of hunger in her stomach. The castle's kitchen had been too busy for her to sneak in. It didn't matter, this wasn't the first time she'd gone hungry and she knew she could push through it.

"Just a little more, Jayne," she whispered, grunting as she slipped her hand over the top ledge. She pushed up and her foot slipped. A small noise escaped her, but she soon righted her hold. "Don't quit."

She pulled her torso over the top to firmer ground and gave a breathless smile of victory. After crawling over the ledge, she rolled onto her back and breathed heavily as she let her muscles rest. The large moon peeked through overhead tree limbs, the leaves crashing in a naturally musical rhythm.

So was this it? The next phase in her life? Were her days as a boxer over? What if the Caniba couldn't help her? What if she could never leave? What would she do?

Ronen instantly came to mind—his strong body and willful charm. For a moment, when he'd touched her, she'd forgotten to think. Even now, in all her tiredness, she felt desire for him. If ever she were to spend a lifetime with a man, he would be a contender. Strength and sexual prowess alone made him a frontrunner. Dominant attitude, while amusing, knocked off a few points.

You are mine.

Had he actually said that? Like she was a piece of property to be owned? The orphanage had thought that way about their charges until one of the kids shoved a metal bar through the workhouse manager's heart.

"Enough dwelling," she scolded her mind. "No weakness. No fear."

The shape of the knife pressed uncomfortably at the small of her back, and she rolled to her hands and knees. He'd never catch her. No one could. She was Jayne "The Sweet" Hart, inter-dimensional boxing champion. She was a fighter and she belonged to no man.

$$\times$$

"You belong to me and I would take what's mine."

Jayne shivered, knowing something wasn't right but not caring. Ronen's soft words washed over her and a hand ran along her calf. The massaging motion felt good after her long run. How had he found her, hidden under thick undergrowth? She'd made sure to brush away her nearby tracks before burrowing into her makeshift bed as the early morning sun peeked through the trees.

"Come back to me."

Jayne moaned. The hand slid up her thigh, firm and confident. She shivered, instantly entranced. Cream wet the folds of her sex and sensational vibrations tingled every inch of her flesh. She found herself wiggling and parting her legs.

Ronen jerked her legs, pulling her roughly from her hiding place. Jayne gasped, reaching to grab the brush to stop herself. Ronen let go. He was alone, kneeling beside her. Sunlight haloed his head, framing his face with light.

"I will have you."

Jayne still didn't speak. She automatically reached for the knife under the brush, but couldn't quite grab it. Ronen's hands were at his waist, fumbling in their eagerness to unlace his breeches. When she tried to move, he grabbed her foot and pulled, sliding her on the forest floor to be close to him.

Ronen managed to free the turgid length of his cock and swallowed it with a strong fist, pumping lightly. With the other hand, he tugged at her tunic to expose her hips. Cool morning air caressed her pussy.

Ronen crawled over her. He grabbed at her neckline, ripping the front of her tunic open. Rough and eager, he feasted on her breasts, licking and sucking the mounds as his hand tested the wetness between her thighs.

Jayne panted and squirmed, gripping his hair. Small twigs and leaves ground into her back, dirtying her hair. His mouth slid from a taut nipple, leaving it wet and suddenly cold. He bit his way to her neck, nipping at her flesh, making her feel his hard kiss.

Urgently, he brought his cock to her sex, finding quick aim before ramming the full length deep into her core. She moaned in pleasure at the almost painful stretching of her muscles. Ronen growled, lifting up so he could pull out only to slam into her like a wild animal. His hips crashed into her, forcing her ass to slide in the dirt.

Jayne liked his vigorous claiming, the swiftness of his thrusts, the confident drive of his passion. She thrust her hand between them, letting his hips bump her fingers against her clit. The stroke sent shivers over her stomach.

Ronen's hair bounced around his tense face with each movement. His neck stretched long and he closed his eyes. Jayne made a weak noise as her orgasm hit. Her body jerked beneath him. He only became more impassioned, pounding her with his cock as she seized and shuddered. Then, suddenly, he made a loud grunt and sheathed himself to the hilt. Release hit and he practically convulsed as he ejaculated inside her.

"You can't hide, my lady, I'm coming for you."

Jayne gasped and blinked, still panting from their joining. She looked around, trying to get a sense of what happened. Ronen was gone, but her body lay soaked in sweat on the forest floor. Though untorn, her tunic was bunched at her waist, revealing the wet evidence of her recent orgasm. Whatever happened, it had been too real to be a dream. Yet here she was, alone.

✕

Ronen gasped for breath, not getting up from where he'd fallen against a tree. Pumping both fists over his exposed cock, he met his climax with a violent jerk. Cum slid over his hands, wetting him as he milked every ounce of pleasure from his body.

He knew the sensations racking him were not a dream. He'd been fully awake when they'd started. But somehow it was more than a fantasy, taking control of his mind, grabbing onto what would have been a fleeting thought about finding Jayne and taking her wildly on the forest floor.

The smell of her surrounded him. He felt the soft globes of her breasts in his mouth when he enveloped them with kisses. He saw her face, felt her body, tasted her flesh.

Witchcraft. Spells. It was the only explanation that made sense. Somehow, Jayne enchanted him. But why? To delay him? Confuse him? Tempt him or drive him mad?

"Ronen, come!" Sorin's voice called. "Kar found her trail going up Boar Ledge."

Springing into action, he fastened his breeches before the others saw what he'd done and went to grab his fallen sword. He'd been searching the ground for her lost trail when the passion struck him. Now, having once again picked up her trail, he leapt onto his horse.

"Stupid woman," he cursed. Why in the name of the gods would she climb up there? The natural jutting of dirt kept the sounder of wild boars that lived on the high plain away from the rest of the forest. Young knights would go there to hunt and practice their survival skills, but it was no place for a woman with only a knife to protect her. The animals grew thick and fat without other natural predators to dwindle their numbers and to kill one would only mean you had a whole pack of them left to go. Even the wolves seemed to avoid it unless desperate during a harsh winter.

When he arrived, Kar already stood on the ledge with Sorin. Ronen reined his horse next to the cliff and climbed onto the animal's back to give him the leverage he needed to reach up. He took his brother's offered hand and jumped off the horse onto the higher ledge. They never brought the horses with them onto the ledge. There was no practical way to get the animals up.

"It leads that way." Kar pointed a scarred finger toward an opened path. He was one of the best trackers in Staria.

"Divide and ride around the ledge," Ronen ordered the knights below them. With luck, she'd have jumped off and continued along a safer route. "We'll meet on the other side."

The men instantly obeyed, splitting into two groups. Three of them grabbed the unused horses' reins to lead them away. Ronen placed his hand on his sheathed weapon and hurried to find Jayne's trail.

SON OF A WHORING CAT!

Jayne leapt over a fallen log, running full tilt through the open forest. The thunder of many small hooves echoed behind her, punctuated by grunts. She'd sprinted into an open clearing of red bristled boars as they routed around in the earth during the morning hours. At least, she was pretty sure that was what they were. She'd slept near an animal collective for a few months when she lived on the streets, and there was a version of the creature kept there in a cage. Only that creature had been much, much smaller than the thirty six-hundred-plus pound hunters behind her.

At first, she hoped to back away slowly from the compact beasts, but her rapid appearance had gotten notice and beady eyes turned toward her in interest. If she weren't mistaken, they actually started salivating. Next, she hoped to startle them by screaming and waving her arms. It had been a mistake. They answered her flailing attempts with loud grunts as they worked their large tusks up and down.

Cursed piglets from the underworld!

The demonic creatures ran pretty fast for their short legs. Jayne leapt, trying to grab a branch to pull herself into a tree. The limb gave under her weight, cracking and refusing to support her. A boar crashed through the brush next to her, trying to ram her thigh. Jayne dodged the attack, but the animal managed to hook her tunic with his tusk. The material ripped. The boar grunted in short, noisy bursts and the sound of hooves shifted in the distance, growing instantly louder.

Jayne reached behind her back to grab the knife, tugging at the hilt. She'd bound it tight so it wouldn't fall or cut her, but now she struggled to free it as she inched away from the boar. Not wanting to face down all of them at once, she again took her chances in fleeing. She gave up on the knife, pumping her arms to propel her body forward. Seeing a formation in the ground, she ran for it and found it led to a steep drop in the forest floor. Looking down over the side, she saw the steep edge looked much like the cliff she had climbed up. The sound of hooves again grew closer.

"Here's hoping you can't fly." Jayne jumped, aiming for a flat spot of earth. But then, a tingling erupted inside her temple and her vision blanked out, replaced the ground with the image of a knight kneeling as he pointed into the distance. She stopped moving, feeling as if she stood perfectly still in the forest even though somewhere in her brain she knew she still fell. Inexplicably, she felt Ronen was close, so close he was almost inside her body, or maybe she was in his.

Suddenly, a hard thud jarred her from her thoughts, bringing her mind back to the present. A sharp pain radiated from where the knife's hilt slammed into her spine. Whatever vision had overtaken her during the fall was now gone.

Jayne moaned, rolling on the ground in agony. Through the corner of her eye she saw the boar, its feet digging into the earth to stop its progress. It was too late. The animal slid right off the side, soaring though the air with a squeal. Forgetting the pain, she jumped to her feet. The animal slammed into the ground, slid several feet before hitting a tree, jerked violently and then held perfectly still.

Reaching for the blade, she tore at the back of her tunic, gasping from her exertions as she finally managed to free the knife. She held it in her trembling hand. Her body throbbed from the fall. Jayne stumbled away from the creature, scanning along the top of the cliff for more. A few boars appeared, grunting in anger, but none followed their friend over the side.

Jayne grabbed the side of her head and pressed down hard. The tingling sensation had lessened, but left her dizzy. Something was very wrong. This was the second time she'd connected to Ronen when he wasn't around.

Then realization hit her. Jayne looked at her fingertip, where she'd poked it with the sword from his bedchamber wall. That's how it must have happened. She'd jabbed her finger, sucked it between her lips and then kissed him. She'd been warned something like this might happen when the Divinity scientists fitted her with the corporation's standard boxer's biogenetics package. But they also said it was a one in a billion chance.

Son of a whoring cat!

Ronen was her one in a billion and she didn't like it one bit.

5

WILD BOAR TASTED ABOUT AS good as it looked running around trying to kill her. Jayne had sliced off the chunk of meat, carried it into the forest and started a small fire in a hand-dug hole. It took a while to get the fire to light, because it had been a long time since she'd used the skill.

"These Caniba better be technological geniuses," she muttered, biting into the overdone meal, trying not to taste it. "I can't live in this forest."

Maybe Lilith had the right idea in staying at the castle. Then again, every ounce of Jayne rebelled at the idea of captivity. She had no choice but to run. Her head began to tingle and she dropped her meat, quickly turning to stare at the ground away from the fire. If Ronen switched sight with her, she'd not let him see anything that would help him track her.

"...*lock her away in a tower*," Ronen's voice filled her head.

"*We lost her tracks, my lords*," an unknown voice broke in, "*but I found evidence of a stampede.*"

"*They found prey*," Lord Sorin answered. "*We follow the stampede.*"

Jayne grabbed her head, shaking it to get the voices out of her mind. She needed to get off this plane. Only then could she be rid of her one-night mistake.

✗

"Caniba," Ronen whispered. The stampede tracks had led them back to the ledge with no sign of Jayne. What they did find horrified him. The Caniba should not be so far north, but only they would devour raw meat. The gnawed boar carcass had been bitten, the bites too round and short to be anything but human.

"Perhaps they are lost," Kar offered. Ronen grabbed his sword, prompting the other two knights to do the same. They scanned the forest in search of their enemy.

"They do not leave their encampments without orders," Sorin said, grimly. "They are spies."

"Lady Jayne is in this forest." Ronen frowned, ignoring the twinge he felt in his gut. He didn't need to look at his brother to know what Sorin was thinking. The Caniba did not treat their female prisoners well. He had to find her, save her, protect her. His arms ached to pull her to his chest and hold her. Why had she run? So soon after choosing to be with him? This was not how he imagined a marriage or a wife.

Already he was connected to her. He felt her like he'd never felt anyone. He detected her lips near his neck and heard her breathing in his ear, or what he imagined to be her breath. The sensation of her body pressed to his, and his cock stayed semi-erect, begging to be called into action. Why hadn't he stayed and made love to her again and again? If he had, maybe she would have been too tired to leave him. If he had, they wouldn't be in the forest looking at evidence of Caniba activity.

The gods have their reasons.

"Here, blood," Kar said, pushing to his feet as he rubbed the found droplet between two fingers. "It has been well over an hour since they passed, perhaps two or three."

"Ronen?" Sorin asked, deferring to him.

"Leave a sign for the others to follow," Ronen ordered. "We follow the Caniba. Nothing else in this forest is as dangerous."

$$\times$$

THE NIGHT SKY didn't give much light as dark clouds drifted over the moon and stars. Jayne saw peeks of moonlight through the treetops and wished she'd brought her fire with her. But, it was better not to signal any surrounding knights. There was no doubt Ronen chased her. What? Did she hurt his male pride? Embarrass him? Why else would he pursue her so far away from the castle?

Whenever she felt Ronen invading her mind, she concentrated on blocking him out. For the most part, it worked. Though, the visions did continue—flashes of forest trees and knights, sounds of voices and running feet.

Darkness and little sleep forced her to find a place to hide for the night. Twice, she almost twisted her ankle because she couldn't see the ground beneath her. Unable to force herself into a tight corner for fear of what would be lurking there, she rolled beneath an overhang of low branches and spread out on her stomach. She laid the knife at her side within easy reach.

Tension rolled through her and she closed her eyes, willing her dreams to be filled with shadows and not sexually fueled fantasies of Ronen. She let the exhaustion have her, slipping easily to sleep.

At first, it was the hands stirring against her naked body that drew her from her slumber. His touch pulled her mind to awareness. Understanding what was happening, she knew she didn't really lie naked, only felt the sensations in her mind as if they were real.

Jayne fought her budding desires, not wanting to give in, but his touch was like a drug. The more she felt, the more she had to have him. Their connection became real, as if he stood in front of her, their minds joining. She actively pushed him from her thoughts, not wanting to let him into her secrets.

She tried to peek into his mind, but all she discovered were random thoughts. *Soft, sweet, mine...*

Jayne felt his possessiveness of her, his drive to capture her. She would never be his prisoner. Never.

Even as she thought it, knowing it to be true, she couldn't resist him. He touched her with such worshiping passion. Palms cupped her breasts, rubbing softly. They ran over her sides, across her hips, down her legs and up her inner thighs. She moaned in torment. How could she resist?

"Please let me go. I can't live as a whore," she whispered. "I wish I'd never met you."

She couldn't see anything, but the darkness only enhanced her other senses. Jayne smelled the freshness of the forest, felt it's coolness on her shoulders and feet. Beneath her, the hard ground pressed into her sore back, but it didn't hurt quite as badly as before. Her nerves focused on Ronen's hands, wanting more of him. He answered her silent plea with his lips, brushing soft kisses over her flesh along the same path his fingers had traveled. Soft breathing washed over her like a gentle breeze.

The moist heat of his mouth enclosed a nipple, sucking the taut peak. She lifted her hands to touch him, but her limbs were heavy as if paralyzed by her sleepy state. Ronen's tight stomach pushed at her thighs, urging them to part as he moved over her. He kissed a trail up her neck, stopping close to her lips.

"Touch me," he said, so softly she barely heard him. Or maybe he didn't speak at all, merely directed the thought into her mind.

Any hint of her resistance left her, and she stopped concentrating on blocking him from her. Almost instantly, her vision began to clear and a moonlit face appeared before her. Thick shadows contrasted the strength of his features and the cords of his neck. The low branches pressed over them, cocooning them in.

Jayne reached for him, grabbing his face to pull his mouth to hers. She gripped him tight, forcing him against her rough kiss. His lips tasted sweet, like fresh water from a spring and she drank thirstily. Her hands acted on their own accord, venturing over the peaks and valleys of his muscles. Restless legs moved along his hips, inviting him to conquer her completely.

Ronen flexed, surging forward. The turgid length of his cock probed the silken heat of her pussy. For a moment, he paused, letting her muscles adjust around him. He worked his body back and forth, going deep with each pass. It felt so good that she wanted to scream with the pleasure of it. Maybe she did scream, but she couldn't be sure.

He thrust hard and fast, as if desperate to mark her as his own. Jayne met his passion, silently battling him for control. The enclosure was too tight for her to roll him onto his back. She raked her nails over his back. Tree limbs scratched at her hands, but she didn't care. Ronen groaned, propelling his body onward.

Jayne gasped, tensing as she met with release. Her quivering muscles gripped his cock and he soon followed, grunting like a wild animal as he came inside her. The sound of their harsh breath joined in a frantic rhythm.

Ronen looked deeply into her eyes, his face still a heavy contrast. "I'm coming for you, Lady Jayne."

Within a blink, his body was gone, leaving her fully clothed and incredibly sated. She panted, wondering how much of her he'd read. Did he know where she hid? Did he understand what happened between them? Just as she started to calm herself, determined to come up with a new plan, her hair was yanked from above and an unknown hand pulled her from beneath her hiding place. Jayne reached for her knife, barely grabbing it only to have it slide from her fingers to be lost in the darkness.

He'd found her.

✕

BLESSED NIGHT.

Ronen shifted on his horse, glad for the cover of darkness to hide the passion he'd just shared with his wife. Spell or not, the woman knew how to sate him. What he didn't understand was why let him join with her as she tried to escape. Several times he thought of telling Sorin, only to refrain. If it was truly believed she was a witch, Jayne would be tried as such. He didn't relish the idea of his wife being burned alive or drowned in a river because of peasant fear. And if it wasn't a spell but the hopeful madness of his own mind, he didn't exactly want the lunacy known.

Automatically, Ronen searched the low branches, remembering the tight fit of Jayne's body to his in the tight enclosure. Sir Traven and Sir Walter had found the mark Ronen and his brother left near the boar's carcass and followed their trail into the forest. Walter rode back to get their horses and now they made good time through the trees. The other knights were deployed to look for signs of Lady Jayne around the ledge.

"Perhaps we should wait for morning light," Traven suggested. "It's too hard to find a trail in such darkness."

Though sensible, it didn't mean Ronen liked the advice.

"You haven't slept, my lord," Kar put forth. "Perhaps you should rest. I will look for a trail by foot."

How could he sleep knowing she was out there? That the Caniba were out there?

"No. I ride. Kar, you three rest and look at first light." Ronen's order ended all discussion from the men. To his brother, he said, "Make up your own mind, but I cannot stop searching."

"You are my blood. I go where you go," Sorin answered. "I ride with you, Brother."

Ronen nodded, having pretty much known Sorin would.

By the wrath of the gods, I have to find her.

✕

JAYNE EXPECTED to see Ronen as moonlight shone over her attacker, but instead she found a wild, furry beast. Light shone through the uncombed nest of its hair. The creature grunted like an evil gorilla that crawled from the depths of a nightmare.

Jayne sprung into action, pushing her legs off the ground to kick at the creature's head. The flat of her foot landed with a hard thud against its neck. Instantly, it let her go. She rolled onto her side, flinching as her back protested the movement. The last kick had irritated the already sore muscles.

Hands gripped her leg and arm, the clawed nails digging into her flesh. They pulled her across the littered forest, slicing her through leaves and twigs.

The debris dug into her stomach, scratching and poking her through the long tunic shirt. The grunts got louder as another beast found hold on her bare calf and began pulling her in the opposite direction.

Jayne didn't make a sound, even as they lifted her from the ground and the pain surged through her body. They tried to rip her in half. She bit her lip, focusing all her energy on jerking her legs together. The two creatures were thrown into each other, hitting their heads. She fell the few inches down onto the ground. Once free, she pushed up, ready to run. More creatures blocked her path, making her stop short of escape.

Blood trickled down her leg and ankle. She hopped lightly, trying not to put weight on her injured limb. Jayne studied her attackers, seeing them more clearly from her new vantage point. They stood like men, only covered in fur. What were they? Wolfmen? Some other kind of creature from the stories told to scare children?

"Back away," she ordered, keeping a deadly calm to her voice. There were eight in all, counting the men she'd hit on the head who still lay unmoving on the ground.

"Fighter," one of the creatures ground out, his voice so gravelly she could barely make out the words. "We will feed her strength to the queen and be rewarded."

Jayne scanned the ground for her knife, but didn't see it. The shadowed figured moved in. She lifted her hands, hopping on one foot as she readied for a death match.

One of the men leapt, claws extended. Jayne pulled to the side, catching his head. She slammed her injured knee up into his face, hearing a crack. He dropped to the ground. Jayne spun, counting down their numbers in her head.

Five remain.

She turned to the side, putting them in front of her. How could she have been caught off guard with the foul stench of them filling her nostrils? The odor was almost unbearable and she tried not to gag.

Two surged at once, wielding long blades. Jayne swung her arms, but they anticipated her move and she missed. A sword bit into her forearm, slicing deep. She yelped in pain. Though she willed her body to keep fighting, it couldn't take much more abuse. She grabbed her arm, falling to her knees. She half expected the creatures to converge upon her with swords. Instead, one grabbed her by her hair and jerked her completely to the ground. He dragged her unceremoniously behind him. The others grabbed their fallen comrades and hoisted them up onto their shoulders to carry them from the forest.

✕

SOMEWHERE BETWEEN THE banging of Jayne's head against a log and the blurry vision of her awakening mind, the smelly men brought her to their encampment. Her entire body itched as it tried to repair itself. The cut on her arm ached terribly, but she knew it would be the first to heal.

A thick leather collar wrapped her neck and another held her waist, keeping her tight against the pole and making it hard to breathe when she moved. Jayne's hands were free and she felt behind her head. They'd hooked her to a low pole, her back straight and her legs sprawled out before her. She shivered, almost dreading the fact they'd kept her alive when first they acted as though they'd tear her apart.

Jayne twisted, trying to discover the source of shuffling feet. She found a pelt-covered man standing with his back to her. Her hands continued to search for an escape, but found no relief from the pole prison.

Taking a deep breath, she held it, endeavoring to ignore her injuries. The beastly man turned to her, whipping his head about. Sunlight illuminated his gruesome features. Jayne gave a loud inhale of surprise, the noise shrill. Sunken eyes stared at her, filled with hatred and something more she couldn't name. Then, he smiled, a horrific look that shook her to the bone. Teeth had been filed into sharp points, creating a mouthful of yellowed fangs. Scars lined his face, not like the Starian men, but purposeful scars that ran deep, as if he cut upon himself in a fit of madness. Some had yet to heal.

Upon seeing her awake, he strode toward her. Jayne tensed, bending her legs. It might break her neck to kick up at him, but she'd rather die fighting than be at this ungodly creature's mercy. The man laughed, grunting low in the back of his throat, keeping well away from her legs. Coming at her from the side, where she could just see him along the edge of her vision, he grabbed her injured arm and began sniffing at the wound. Metal-tipped fingers dug into her skin, drawing fresh blood. Jayne tried to pull away, but it only caused him to twist it at an awkward angle.

"Leave her!" another of the men yelled. His right nostril had been sliced off. By the way the sniffer dropped her arm and backed away, she guessed him to be the leader. "She is for the queen. Sorceress

Magda will feed on her strength and she will reward us well."

"Sorceress Magda," they all murmured in reverent unison, revealing there to be more of these men out of her eye line.

Feed?

Jayne gulped. For the first time since running from Battlewar Castle, she hoped Ronen would catch her. Closing her eyes, she concentrated on connecting to him. Unfortunately, with her injuries, it would be nearly impossible. Her energy would be used to heal herself.

Bloody fucking misery! I give up. You want me, Ronen, well come and save my ass.

RONEN CLUTCHED the jeweled knife Jayne had stolen from him, swearing to himself that he'd find the Caniba and rip them of their hearts. He'd found the weapon in the dirt, surrounded by signs of a struggle. The trail had been easy enough to find. They simply followed the drag marks and droplets of blood leading away from the original fray south through the woods.

It always amazed him that the Caniba could

survive as a race for as long as they had. They had little by way of tactical skill, not bothering to hide their tracks or plot intricate battles. If not for their leaders, they'd be a mindless army running haphazard across the countryside. Only by killing the leaders would the Caniba tribes fall. Unfortunately, it was not so easily done. The sheer number of the tribe kept anyone from getting too close.

Ronen lifted his hand, hearing a noise in the distance. The distinctive grunts confirmed his worst fears. His enemy had captured his wife. He listened for signs of her screams, but only met with silence. Closing his eyes, he tried to connect with her as he had before. Nothing.

Almost desperate, he gripped the reins of his horse. Pain stung him, seizing hold of his heart. He'd only had one night with her before she ran off, and it seemed strange that he'd already feel so connected to her. Looking at his brother, he thought of Bianka. Why had the gods cursed the brothers of Firewall? They fought every battle put before them, as had their ancestors. Why take their wives in such a cruel way?

Ronen refused to analyze the emotions whirling around inside of him, telling himself that it was merely duty and honor that made him feel anything for Jayne. Despite his hopes, he knew that it was unlikely she lived. The Caniba rarely took prisoners and a scouting party would be less likely to, for they would never see the tactical advantage in doing so.

Ronen grabbed his sword, silently prompting Sorin and Kar to do the same. The others had not caught up with them, but it didn't matter. The Caniba spies had taken his wife and his honor demanded blood. His rage demanded it. He needed to fight, to kill the ache burning his chest and pounding inside his head.

Sorin gave him a stiff nod, agreeing to battle. Kar swung off his horse and inched in front of them, disappearing into the forest. Seconds later, a soft chirp sounded, blending in with the forest noise. It pulsed six times indicating six enemies.

Ronen nudged his steed, ducking under a branch as he surged toward the Caniba encampment. Seeing movement, he rode for the first man he found, hollering to get his attention. The man-creature drew his sword to fight, but Ronen was too enraged to make much sport of it. He sliced the man up the chest, killing him instantly. The others sprung into action, leaping up from their spots on the ground.

"Ronen!" Sorin yelled, drawing his notice. "Your wife!"

Ronen stiffened, searching the campground. Sorin pointed at a low pole. Jayne's back was to him, but he could see her feet kicking at the ground as if she'd push the pole over. It didn't budge but she kept trying.

She lives! He couldn't believe it.

"Take her out of here!" Sorin ordered, his desperation to save his sister-by-marriage a mere droplet compared to Ronen's desire to save his wife. Sorin slashed at an attacker, beheading him. Ronen knew his brother could handle himself and did as he instructed, turning his mount toward the post. Kar appeared from the forest on foot, meeting swords. The clang of metal against metal echoed around them.

Ronen jumped from his horse, landing with a thud next to Jayne. Her entire body jerked at the sound. His eyes went first to the blood and dirt marring her flesh, searching for injuries. Her body was covered with them.

Light brown eyes met his. He expected there to be terror in her gaze, or even tears. Instead, she looked incredibly annoyed at having been captured.

"My lady, did they...?"

"Took you long enough," she muttered, struggling anew. "Mind cutting me free?"

"You wished for me to find you? Is that why you ran? Because of a game?" He frowned. Though the idea gave him hope. Ronen pulled the jeweled knife from his waist and began sawing at the leather straps keeping her to the post. The collar around her neck would have to come later.

"You really want to discuss this now?" she snapped. "Here?" Jayne reached for his hands to take over freeing herself. He swatted her away.

Ronen glanced up at the fight. All but one Caniba had fallen. Sorin faced him on foot. Kar stood back, turning in circles as he searched the trees for more.

"Finally," Jayne said as she broke free. She pushed the leather band from her waist as she stood, ready to charge into battle. The action came too fast and she swayed on her feet, nearly collapsing on top of him. Ronen stood, catching her. "Let go. I'm fine!"

"Never," he growled, forcing her to walk with him as he hurried to his horse. "Get on."

"No," she denied. Though the sound was hard, there was a deep terror in her eyes that he'd never seen before. His wife was a fighter. He already knew that. But now, when she looked at him, it was almost as if he terrified her more than the idea of facing the forest alone. "I will not be told what to do. I can take care of myself."

"Is that what you call this? Taking care of yourself?" Ronen snorted in disbelief. She looked at him, her eyes wide. If he didn't know better, he would have thought he'd deeply hurt her feelings by pointing out her capture.

"I..." Jayne looked at the pole where she'd been tied. He could practically see her mind ticking away in her skull, trying to decide what to do, how to react.

"Get on the horse, my lady." He lowered his tone to a deadly pitch, hoping to jar her into action. Men would not disobey such a harsh command. This lady did.

"No," she stated loudly. Her eyes moved from him to the dead bodies on the ground. He'd seen that look before in young soldiers—the shock, the disbelief. Dazed, she said, "I can walk."

"Do not refuse help for the sake of being stubborn. Get on the—" Ronen jerked her hard, trying to get her to focus, needing her to snap back to her senses.

Jayne pulled her arm roughly from his grasp. Her voice rose as she yelled at him, "Stop telling me what to do. I'm tired of people telling me what to do. Because I'll tell you right now, I don't take kindly to being commanded or tied up or made to..."

"Ronen!" Sorin yelled. "Get her out of here. Now! We scout the forest and will meet you at Widowrock."

"I am not commanding you, I am protecting you." All right, so that was half true.

Jayne frowned. Despite her bruised and bloodied body, and the fact she stood in the aftermath of a miniature battlefield, she managed to look defiant. "I'm not yours to protect. I'm not your mate."

"Fine, breeding partner, wife, whatever you wish to call yourself." How was it he wanted to pull her to his chest and strangle her at the same time? Why did she fight him so hard when all he wanted was to hold her? Protect her? Emotions warred within him. He'd searched for her with little rest, and all he wanted to do was lock her away in a room with him where she would be safe. Maybe he'd leave the collar around her neck and tie her to a bed until she saw reason. "You are mine. I am yours. We are together."

"You can hang yourself." She began clawing at her neck, trying to get the leather off. It was then he realized what was truly happening. She fought with him because she didn't know how else to react. It was as if accepting his help admitted some kind of failure on her part. The reasoning wasn't logical, not by Starian standards. It was then Ronen also realized he knew so very little about his wife's past. He trusted the gods, trusted fate, but there was something more, something deeper to Jayne.

Was it possible he'd found a woman whose instinct to fight was stronger than any Starian man's? Ronen wouldn't pretend to understand tender, romantic feelings, but he knew women by nature were not usually so unwilling to accept friendship. But with the way Jayne was looking at him, it appeared she would be much more comfortable facing death than being with him as a wife.

"I belong to no one and the only thing we'll be doing together is—"

Ronen refused to listen to any more. Understanding her nature a little bit better did not lessen the danger of their situation. He grabbed her and tossed her across the back of his horse so her stomach lay over the saddle. The animal pawed the ground, snorting softly. Until Kar and Sorin had a chance to secure the surrounding woods, he couldn't risk keeping her out in the open.

He swung up behind her, perched uncomfortably on the saddle's edge. Jayne growled in protest, trying to push up with her one good arm. Pressing his hand to her back, he kept her down as he spurred the mount into action. It was a short ride to Widowrock and, so long as she didn't struggle, she wouldn't be dangling for too long.

"Let me up, you son of a whoring cat!" she screamed.

"We ride to safety." He kept his hand on her. "And my mother was a gracious and good lady. You'd do well not to insult her again."

Jayne mumbled an answer, but he didn't make out the words.

6

"Tell me something. Battlewar Castle, it's not a brothel, is it? A whorehouse? Gathering place for prostitutes?" Jayne stared at Ronen, willing him to fight with her. She could handle fighting. Being weak was another story. Besides, if he fought her, she wouldn't have to face that protective, almost gentle look on his face. How was a woman supposed to react to that? No one in her entire life looked at her the way he did. No one made her feel the way he did. Death she could manage and face. But this tenderness? It terrified her like nothing else had.

Ronen frowned, pausing as he swung from the back of his horse to look down at her. "No. It's the king's castle. The king doesn't stay there as there is always too much to do by the borderlands, but we use it for ceremonies and such."

So much for that theory. I think I might prefer a brothel to marriage. When Jayne looked at Ronen, she wasn't so sure she really believed that.

"You know, where I come from a man goes through certain rituals before asking a woman to marry him, and then they only cohabitate for ten years. If, at the end of that time, they want to file for another ten they can." Jayne hated feeling weak, but she'd pushed her body hard the last several days on little food. She could take the pain, even the hunger, but she couldn't take the fact that it had all been for nothing. Ronen had caught up to her. So what if he'd saved her life in the process. It didn't mean he planned on letting her go.

No, he thought she belonged to him. What was worse, he didn't consider her to be a slave or prisoner. No, to him she was a mate, a breeding partner, a wife. Out of all those names, wife scared her the most. Though, breeding partner did take a close second. Too bad for him, the biogeneticist assured her she would never have children. Divinity wouldn't want a pregnant boxer waddling around the ring.

"Here we mate until death," he answered. He turned his back on her and busied himself clearing a spot on the forest floor. He wore a different tunic than she'd last seen him in, but his eyes belied his exhaustion. The barest hint of whiskers textured his jaw, darkening the already tanned flesh. Bloody misery, the man knew how to move—from the strength in his chest and arms to the almost graceful rhythm of his walk.

Jayne went to a big boulder standing by itself in the middle of the forest, completely isolated from other rocks. Widowrock, they'd called it. On impulse, she braced her shoulder against it and tried to push it in his direction, grunting, "If you insist."

The boulder didn't budge. Ronen gave her a bemused glance, dismissing her idle threat. "Come sit before you hurt yourself. Let me take that collar off your neck."

"Shouldn't you go check on your brother? What if he is hurt?" She stayed against the rock, leaning against it. Even with tired eyes, Ronen was a stunning man. Their joined fantasies were never far from her thoughts. Though unreal, they felt quite the opposite. Funny how she'd made love to him more in her dreams than in real life. "Don't worry, I'll be sure to wait right here."

"For me to consider his defeat would be a dishonor," Ronen answered, crossing to her.

Argh! She hated his calm tone. She wished he would scream, yell, punch. That language she understood.

"Turn. I'll free you." He urged her head to the side with a gentle shove before taking the knife to her neck. The sharp blade soon had her free.

Jayne grabbed her neck, stretching the muscles. He stepped back and she watched in silence as he gathered dried leaves, branches and twigs to build a fire. Within minutes, a soft firelight cast over them.

"Let me see your arm." He stood, reaching his hand out for her to join him.

"It's fine." Jayne didn't like the softness in his gaze. Why wasn't he yelling at her for running away?

"You're wounded. I should bind it."

"It's already healing." She refused his comfort.

"Why must you make a battle of this?" he muttered, more to himself.

Jayne answered anyway. "If you don't like it, let me go."

"What is it that makes you want to fight and face death rather than accept me? You chose me. I was content to not claim a woman. It was you who bewitched me with your kiss." He strode toward her, closing the distance. Placing his hand on the rock, he leaned into her. "It is you who has been plaguing my mind with thoughts of taking you. We are connected. We are meant to be."

"We are joined by defective nanobots." She sighed heavily, letting him hear her frustration. "When I cut my finger on your sword and stuck it between my lips—"

"I remember," he interrupted needlessly. His tone dropped to a low whisper.

Jayne continued, trying to ignore the sultry dip of his lashes and the parting of his firm lips. "When we kissed—"

"Yea." His breath fanned over her cheek.

"One of them left my bloodstream and somehow took up residence in you. Since they're programmed to work as a team with my body, they've decided to talk to each other from inside our bodies." She leaned away from him, but the small distance did nothing to quell her growing arousal. "I was warned it might happen, but it was supposed to be a one in a million chance. Bloody misery, perhaps even one in a trillion."

Jayne frowned. It was why boxers took a special supplement before a fight so they didn't risk transferring their technologies.

"See, we are blessed by the gods." He tried to press his lips to hers.

Jayne jerked back another inch. Her resistance didn't seem to faze him. "How is it you hear about a scientific catastrophe and think it's a sign of true love?"

"I confess, I have no idea what manner of spell a nanobot is or what purpose they serve. But if it proves my point that we are meant to be, then I agree with them."

She scowled. "I've got news for you, warrior man, true love doesn't exist. It's an illusion."

"I agree."

That surprised her. With all his "mine" mentality, she just thought he'd be a romantic of sorts. He spoke of the "will of the gods" and "meant to be". She wondered why she felt disappointment at his cold, logical admission—an admission she said first.

"It is not in our nature to seek romantic love. Marriages are unions, partnerships. Women must be cared for and protected, provided for. Men need sons and," he brushed his finger over her cheek, "the pleasure of a woman's bed."

Jayne swallowed nervously. She didn't necessarily like the life he laid out before them. What if she couldn't escape it? Or him? Or this barbaric place? What if she didn't want to?

"It is my hope we will find a mutual affection in

time," he continued, not taking his eyes from hers. "Marriages seem the better for it."

"I want you to listen to me, Ronen," she said, quietly, reasonably. Mutual affection? How could she make him understand that everyone who felt any kind of affection for her was dead? That it was better for both of them if they went their separate ways? "Do you really want a woman who was sent here as a punishment?"

"Punishment?" He dropped his hand. "You are a criminal? Traitor?"

"I'm a loser," she stated flatly. For all Divinity cared, it was the truth. She'd lost her fight, even if it was fixed.

"What did you lose? Something important? A king's missive?" He furrowed his brow, as if trying to think of all the lost things that warranted a punishment.

"My championship title to the cheating, son of an ape, Big Bobby Bishop in the gladiator rings on dimensional plane 241." Jayne felt angry all over again and pushed off the rock. "His gangster father tried to make me throw the fight, but there is no way I could take a dive to that no-talent buffoon." She paced across the forest floor. "They threatened to kill my family if I didn't fall. Well, my nonexistent family but they didn't know that. And the son of a whoring cat hits me with a whammy?! I let him beat on me for a half an hour to make a good show and to let him have a little dignity when he lost, and he drugs me. Me! Jayne 'The Sweet' Hart."

"I do not understand what this has to do with you as my wife." Ronen hadn't moved.

"I don't lose. I never lose. Divinity Corporation banks on that, and they've paid a lot of doctors a lot of money to make sure of it. When Big Bobby hit me with his drugged fist, a lot of money was lost by a lot of powerful people. Divinity would not have been happy about it and they were my way home. But instead of hearing my side, they packed me up and shipped me off to this forsaken..." She paused, trying to think of a description that wasn't as mean as the ones filtering through her head. "Ah, place."

"So you fight for money?" He looked over her in disbelief. "You do not look like a warrior. I have seen your body. The skin is smooth. There are no scars."

"Bare-knuckle boxing." Jayne looked down at her arm where the deep gash already began to heal. She held it up to show him. "I've been bioengineered to heal fast and not to scar. It keeps my face pretty for the fans."

He looked down at his body. "I have that thing. I will no longer scar?"

"Nano-robots are these tiny, microscopic, self-sufficient army of machines designed to replicate and act on a specific level of function while they travel around my bloodstream to heal my body. They're engineered to only work on me. But somehow one of my nanobots jumped ship and is inside of you. It should have deactivated."

"But the gods willed that we—"

"Ah," Jayne held up her hand stopping him from saying it. "Scientific mishap. With any luck you'll bleed the bugger out and the air will deactivate it. Then it's bye-bye shared thoughts. Or your own immune system will attack it and shut it down."

"No part of me could attack you, Lady Jayne."

Jayne got the distinct feeling he didn't under-stand half of what she said.

Ronen grabbed her hand and jerked her forward into his chest. The hard press of his muscles formed a solid wall. He turned her back against the boulder, trapping her. The unmistakable press of his erection made itself known. "I enjoy the shared thoughts." He rocked his hips. "And when I feel your sex clutching my cock as you finish, I know you enjoy them as well."

"I don't deny that there is, ah," she chose her words carefully, "sexual lust."

"We have time before the others arrive." He rocked again, swaying his hips back and forth. "And it is said any lady who makes love to her husband against Widowrock will never be named a widow."

"I don't believe in legends." Her breathing deepened. Every part of her body tingled, from the top of her head, the pointed buds of her nipples, the tight pearl of her clit, the slick folds of her sex, to the very tips of her toes. She couldn't think or reason, not when his delicious mouth was so close. Sex wouldn't change anything between them. He'd still demand she was his wife. She'd still try to find a way to escape.

Jayne grabbed his face and roughly pulled his mouth down to slam against hers. She bit at his lips, kissing him with a potent force. Ronen didn't seem to mind when she raked her hands over his tunic, jerking it up so she could free his thick cock. When she couldn't figure out how to unfasten his breeches, he helped her, tugging them so they loosened enough for her to reach down the front. She grabbed his rigid shaft, pumping it in a tight fist.

Ronen groaned, squeezing a breast. He whispered hotly against her throat, "Lift your skirts, my lady. I would take you now."

Jayne wanted to be in control. She let go of his cock and pushed him down. "On your back so I can mount you, Knight."

"Yea, my lady, whatever you wish." He scurried to obey, his breathing deepening in his eagerness to be ridden. Ronen pulled his breeches down, exposing his cock in readiness for her.

"My wish is to ride you." Jayne was hardly embarrassed by such admissions. She climbed over him, lifting the long tunic to bare her pussy. "Hard and rough until you beg me for mercy."

"I am not accustomed to begging." He gripped her bare hips, forcing her up against his cock. "But my lady is welcome to try."

Jayne grabbed him by the hair and lifted him up to meet her mouth. She kissed him hard, sawing her lips against his. The heat of his thighs teased her sex and she squirmed, undulating her hips.

Something about him drove her to distraction and she lost all logical thought. Knowing this was real this time and not just an overactive fantasy, spurred Jayne on. She needed him. Now.

Jayne dropped his head, lifting her body over him. Ronen took his cock in hand, guiding it to her as her fingernails dug into his tunic. She impaled herself on him, gasping at the pleasure of his thick probe. Warm, strong hands skimmed her thighs and hips, touching but not controlling.

Ronen moaned. Jayne found herself going slow despite her earlier decree. She savored each thrust, each sway. Rocking her hips in small circles, she found the perfect rhythm. She ran her fingers along his chiseled face, across the rough texture of a whiskered jaw. He trapped one between his lips, sucking gently.

Tension built, propelling her onward. Ronen managed to find her naked breasts beneath the shirt and cupped her so her erect nipples flattened against his palms. Jayne quickened her tempo until she slammed into him. Pleasure crashed over her, making her tense and shake. She inhaled deeply, her pussy quivering violently around his cock. Ronen still moved beneath her, taking shallow thrusts before finally exploding to join his release with hers.

Jayne rolled off him, falling onto her back. Her muscles still ached, but sex had done wonders to relax them. Inside, it felt as if her bones turned water and every nerve was numbed with the euphoria of the aftermath.

Ronen tugged at his breeches next to her, lacing

them along the hip. "I am glad you have accepted your role as my wife. I promise you will not regret it."

His words caused an ache deep in her chest. Didn't he understand what this was?

"I don't need a man's protection," she whispered. "I can take care of myself."

"You are strong," he agreed, "and will bring much honor to our family name, my Lady of Firewall."

"I don't think you understand. I have no need of a husband. I never wanted one." She didn't move beyond tugging her tunic over her exposed hips to hide them from view. "As for your reasons, I cannot fulfill them. I can't give you children. I won't keep your house. I hate cleaning up after other people. I won't feed you. All that leaves you with is a whore to see to your needs. Surely paying a prostitute is cheaper than keeping a wife."

Ronen visibly paled. Weakly, he said, "We have servants."

Jayne turned away from him, rolling her eyes in disbelief. Really? That's all he had to say? Servants? As if that solved all her issues and would suddenly make her want to be with him forever. She decided long ago that she wasn't one for marriage and family. Sitting on the ground, she gingerly pushed at her wounded arm, resisting the urge to scratch the healing tissue.

"I hear my brother," Ronen said, breaking the uneasy silence. He pushed up from the ground, hitting the dust from his clothes. Seconds later she heard the sound of horses' hooves. Lord Sorin wasn't alone, and when he rode into the clearing around Widowrock, fourteen knights came with him.

Moody eyes turned toward her. She arched a brow, forcing all emotion from her face as she stared back. Why were they mad at her? She didn't ask them to hunt her down.

"Maps," Sorin stated, looking at his brother. He held up a fur pouch. His hand was covered with blood.

"Watch my lady," Ronen told the men, automatically following his brother without a backward glance.

Jayne sighed heavily, letting the knights see her irritation. Muttering to herself, she turned her back on them and sat down by the boulder. "Fourteen guards, my lord? Do you really think that will stop me?"

RONEN WAS grateful for his brother's interruption. He still didn't know what to say to his wife. No children? It would be a lie to say the news wasn't disappointing. He wanted children very much—sons to carry on the family name and tradition, a daughter to bless their home. When she talked it was clear Divinity had done some diabolical things to her—nanobots and bioengineering? He didn't fully understand what those things were, but the way her arm healed was not natural. Is that why she couldn't give them children?

"Ronen?" Sorin frowned. "Do I have your mind?"

"Yea," Ronen lied. He hadn't been listening.

Sorin held up the pouch. "We found this on the Caniba spies. They are mapping routes through the forest originating at Spearhead."

"Magda," Ronen ground out.

"The Sorceress plans something." Sorin pulled out a piece of parchment and dropped the Caniba pouch on the ground. "We must warn King Wilhelm so he can order troops to reinforce the borderland marshes. His personal army should be camped near Daggerpoint Castle."

"I will go," Ronen stated. "You must go back to your wife."

Sorin's face darkened. "Be sure the king knows I'm ready to march."

"Is the choice so bad?" Ronen grabbed the parchment and slid it beneath his tunic, holding it in place beneath his belt.

"Battles are nothing compared to what she puts me through," Sorin answered. Ronen knew it was all the explanation he'd receive. But, he really didn't need words. By the look in his brother's face, Lady Lilith denied him her company and her bed. Should it continue, it would make for a hard marriage and a miserable life for his brother.

Ronen thought of Jayne. It would seem the Lords of Firewall both had problems. "Trust in the gods, my brother. They do not give us trial without reason."

"Yea." Sorin instantly changed the subject. "I'll take most of the men back to Battlewar and leave four to scour the forest to ensure no more spies linger. I'll spread word in the village that Lady Jayne's departure was the will of the gods and she led us to the spies."

"Yea, and I'll take Kar and Lance. There might be need of a healer on the battlefront." Ronen held out his hand. "Journey smooth and swift."

"Fight well," Sorin answered, grasping his hand

before striding back to where the men awaited their orders.

Ronen was glad for an excuse to avoid Battlewar Castle. Not only would the battlefront distract his mind, but it was far away from the only Divinity portal in the land and Jayne's only way out of his dimensional plane. By the will of the fire goddess, she would never have the chance to leave him again.

✕

JAYNE WATCHED in surprise as the knights rode off after Lord Sorin. They'd only left her with two guards—albeit large, disapproving, intimidating guards. She interlaced her fingers, cracking her knuckles. Yeah, she was pretty sure she could take them.

Jayne made no move to leave the boulder. The guards had horses and trying to outrun them would be a futile effort, even if she were to knock them unconscious first. They'd already proved apt at tracking through the forest, and if her recent beastly captors were any indication, she couldn't rely on help from the Caniba.

Technologically advanced race?

Jayne chuckled at the thought. The knights

137

frowned in her direction at the sound. She laughed harder.

"What has happened?" Ronen strode through the forest.

"She's gone mad," a knight answered. He was the one from her joined vision with Ronen who'd been hunting her in the forest.

"Methinks she is overtired," the third knight said, a redheaded man with steady eyes and a thoughtful expression. "Do we ride back to Battlewar?"

"No. We go to Daggerpoint to seek an audience with the king." Ronen strode to his horse and swung up into the saddle. Then, walking the animal toward her, he held out his hand. Jayne hesitated, gauging the jump up. Finally, too exhausted to argue, she grabbed his wrist. Ronen jerked, pulling her up. It wasn't her most graceful landing, but she managed to slide behind him on the saddle. It didn't seem to take much for her body to respond to his nearness. With her legs apart and the tight space holding them firmly together, her sex molded to his ass as her thighs pressed into his. He spurred the horse into a gait and her breasts bounced against his back. Jayne closed her eyes, trying not to get aroused.

This ride is already too long.

7

ONE LONG NIGHT of travel had been made even more so by the way her body rubbed up against Ronen's. The horse rocked in a steady, yet somewhat dizzying rhythm. Jayne tried to stay awake, but the forest was endless and the warmth of Ronen's back so inviting. Before she realized it, she had her arms lazily wrapped around his hips and her cheek pressed into him in sleep.

By the time she awoke, dawn streaked the horizon, illuminating a valley filled with caramel-colored square tents. They varied in sizes, spread out over the distance and towered over by a dark gray castle. The larger tents were closest to the castle gate with progressively smaller ones fanning away. Bright banners hung from the tent flaps, pinned to the opened entryways.

Daggerpoint Castle lived up to its name. Tall, smooth spires pointed into the magenta heavens, reaching into sharp points. Banners fluttered in the wind, and Jayne felt sorry for the person who had to climb up that daunting height to affix the things.

"Is this where the king lives?" Jayne asked, forced to grab Ronen's hips as he steered the horse down an incline.

"This is his camp, but he'll be staying inside the castle." Ronen tensed as she held him, and remained stiff. "Battlewar is his home, but he spends more time near the borderlands.'

"Will we stay in the camp?" Jayne hoped so. The soft clang of sword practice echoed around the shouts of laughter coming from a group of men surrounding a couple of bare-chested brutes wrestling in the dirt. The fresh air and unrestrictive prison of tent canvas seemed a far cry better than a dark stone tower.

"If there is a castle nearby, noble ladies stay within." Ronen kept riding, taking a cleared path toward the castle gate. Several men lifted their hands in greeting, shouting welcome and inquiring after Lord Sorin. They didn't speak to her, but they watched her curiously.

"My lord?" Kar appeared at their side.

"Yea," Ronen answered, apparently already knowing what the man wanted. "Take your leave, clean up, drink. Find me after you have rested."

Kar and Lance, the redhead, turned to ride down into the center of camp. They disappeared behind a blue-bannered tent.

"Is there a queen?" Jayne craned her neck to look up at the highest dagger spire. Pointed lancet windows were much wider than the narrow slits of Battlewar Castle. An orange glow shone from within a few of them.

"Why?"

"Because I'm hoping he's without a mate. I wish for more power," she drawled wryly.

"Yea, there is a queen." Ronen grunted. "Besides, noblewomen do not take multiple husbands, only peasants."

Jayne almost said, "lucky them", but refrained. She doubted the moody Lord Ronen would appreciate her dry humor. "I don't see why they'd want more than one."

"Because you don't even want one?" he filled in.

Yeah, Lord Moody all right.

"Can we have a conversation or do I have to shove your ill-tempered ass off this horse?" Jayne gave him a small push. "Tell me about the peasants. Do they get into fights over whose turn it is to do the wife? Because from what I saw of their behavior in Battlewar's many hallways, husbands appear to be very, ah, what's a delicate way of putting this? Hornier than a sex-crazed maniac on hormones." Just to mess with him and amuse herself, she lowered her tone ever so slightly to a sultry, breathy whisper. "Or do the other husbands watch as they each take turns?"

Ronen shifted on his horse. Jayne tried not to laugh.

"I do not know what happens in their bedchambers. I suppose each marriage pact is different," he answered. Then, before she could plant more deliciously inappropriate images into his head, he rushed on, "The arrangement is necessary for poorer families."

"Why?" she whispered against the back of his ear. If everyone insisted on staring at her, she'd give them something to look at—Lord Ronen squirming in his seat while she smiled innocently behind him. "Are peasant women insatiable? Ravenous?"

"Poorer families n-need," he stuttered, "to work together so no one starves and all, um, in the family trade."

She squeezed his hip. "Have you ever wanted to be a peasant? Just throw away the restrictions of your position and join in the naughty group games?"

"Honor forbids I give up my title." The words were final.

"But you don't even fantasize that you're someone else?" She brushed her breasts to his back, unsure why she tried to exasperate him. "I don't see a lot of women in this camp. Those long winter nights have to get pretty lonely. It would only be natural if you—"

"I understand what you are asking." His back relaxed some. "Men who chose the solitary path are not looked down upon, but I am not one of them. I enjoy the company of women. During campaigns, the camp followers make their rounds to see to the needs of the men."

It was Jayne's turn to stiffen. That was *not* what she'd been asking.

"They are more than willing to play out the fantasies of—"

"Hey, just because they're royalty, I won't be expected to bow, will I?" she broke in, changing the suddenly irritating subject. If she wasn't mistaken, he chuckled softly. A jealous wave of possessiveness washed over her. She did not want to hear about him and other women. Sure, she didn't think he came to her bed an untried virgin, but that didn't mean she wanted full details of his past.

"No, women curtsey."

Jayne put space between them. "Maybe you shouldn't introduce me then. I don't do too well with authority. Besides, I'd rather take a bath."

It had taken Ronen a moment to figure out what Jayne meant to do with her questioning about peasants. Her obvious jealousy amused as it assuaged his male vanity. If she thought trying to poke at him until he exploded was wise, then he'd just have to show her that he could poke back.

At first, he nearly jerked her around the front of the horse for a sound, hard spanking. How dare she indicate she wanted more lovers? Ronen refused to share what was his.

He shifted his hips, trying to adjust his heavy erection into a more comfortable position. Even in his initial aggravation, her sultry voice had stirred his blood to boiling. Having those soft breasts bouncing against him had been agony, and it didn't take much to convince his knight to prepare for battle.

Ronen mentally felt for the map at his hip. Duty demanded he hand it over first thing, before bathing or eating. However, after that, he'd be free to whisk his pretty bride to a bedchamber for the rest of the day.

Ronen passed through the low gates of Daggerpoint before motioning to a page. The young boy ran to gather the lord's horse as Ronen hopped down. He reached for Jayne, noting how very unsuitable she was for a formal introduction. The king would understand, but the queen tended to expect more of her noble ladies—regardless of the circumstances.

"I wasn't joking," Jayne said as her feet hit the dirt. "If you make me meet anyone right now, I will embarrass you."

"Your absence will be understood," he promised her, unsure whether her threat should entertain or anger him. "I will have the servants bring you to a sleeping chamber where you can bathe and eat. It would be better for you if you greet the queen with a fresh face."

"Whatever," she dismissed, unimpressed by the fact that royalty was so close. He'd seen women freeze up and faint at the sight of His and Her Majesty. "I just want to lie down."

✕

JAYNE GROANED for the thirteenth time in one minute as she pushed an overly soapy washcloth along her arms. Steam rolled around her from the stone tub, clinging to the warped lead plate windows surrounding three sides of the raised platform of the bath. She'd slicked her damp hair back on her head while keeping all but her face submerged in liquid heat. The dark blue of the water trailed her skin like wet sapphires whenever she lifted her arms from their depths.

"If I never leave this bath again, it will be too soon," she said more to herself than the two servants watching her from where they put fresh linens on the large bed. She felt their eyes on her when they thought she wasn't paying attention. "If you two don't stop staring, I'll order you both to strip naked and await my lord's punishment. He seems the type to be fond of spankings."

Both women gasped in unison and ran from the room. Jayne pushed up far enough to peek at the bed. They'd left the top coverlet halfway off the side. Laughing hard, she sank into the water once more to enjoy the fact she was finally alone.

Closing her eyes, she debated whether or not to

fall asleep right where she lay. Or maybe she'd stir the remnants of desire still lingering from being pressed to Ronen all night. Before she could decide if the risk of drowning outweighed comfort, a small tingling erupted along her temple. She opened her eyes, recognizing the sensation. Her mind was trying to connect her thoughts with Ronen's.

Still irritated by the idea of him and other women, Jayne decided to let it. Unless his meeting with the king only lasted a few short minutes, he'd still be talking to His Majesty. Smiling mischievously, she saw a flash of Ronen's hands around a drink. Instead of exploring his mind, she opened hers.

Grabbing the soapy cloth, she pushed to her knees so she could kneel in the water. Cooler air surrounded her, causing her nipples to harden into two erect points. She ran the cloth up the center of her chest, squeezing it so soap ran over her breasts as she watched. Suds clung to peaks before dripping into the water.

✕

"THE MAP DOES NOT GO TOO DEEPLY into the forest. The beasts could not have been exploring long," King Wilhelm said, scratching his short blond beard. The main hall was empty except for the occasional servant. Queen Patricia had left them to attend the duties of lady of the castle. She liked her world to be organized in a particular way, and Daggerpoint had no official mistress to see to its daily demands.

"My brother has sent men to scout the forest to make sure none live to tell the Sorceress of their discoveries." Ronen didn't move in his seat, well aware of how dirty he must have appeared, covered in dirt and sweat. He needed a bath and a bed, desperately.

"And you're sure it is Sorceress Magda who sends the spies?"

Ronen curled his nose in disgust. "Yea, when they died they shouted the praises of their queen. It is Sorin's and my opinion that we should order troops to reinforce the borderland marshes at Spearhead. He says his men are ready to march at your command."

"We'll increase the forest patrols," Wilhelm said. "I will write to Lord Sorin and have him arrange it from Battlewar. And I will send a messenger to Spearhead for a report."

Ronen nodded, seconds away from pushing up

from his chair to take his leave when the king's words stopped him.

"I am pleased to hear the brothers of Firewall have taken brides."

Ronen didn't answer. He didn't want to speak of his wife. Talking about her would make him think about her. Thinking about her would make him want her. Wanting her would only add fire to his already heavy cock, and the last thing he felt like wearing before the king was a giant erection.

"I know there were many who were hesitant with the alliance, but your example will go far in encouraging other men to take these otherworlders as brides." The king motioned a servant to refill their drinks. "How are the foreign women? Are they of good stock? Are they all Divinity promised?"

"No," he stated flatly. It served no purpose to lie to the king. Wilhelm's eyes rounded in surprise.

"Are they uncomely?"

Ronen drew his eyes to the far side of the hall in the direction of Jayne. "They are most beautiful, but the agreement was for willing brides."

"Is the Lady Jayne not willing?" The king gave him a wry look. "It would explain your dark mood."

"I believe the foreign women might not have known about coming here. They were not awake when they arrived, and Divinity transport insisted we put them into a cell while they adjusted to the new dimension. Two of the five had to be sent back as unsuitable. They were crying hysterically and dishonoring themselves before they even made it to the ceremony. They were given the philter and unhappily returned." Ronen wrinkled his nose in distaste. "It is said one offered to pleasure anyone we put in front of her without consideration in return."

"They sent a camp follower as a bride? That was not in the agreement They were to be agreeable to monogamy." The king paused while the maid filled his cup. He gave her an absent smile.

When the maid finished with his goblet, Ronen reached to take a drink. He blinked, seeing a flash of soft, wet flesh reflected back at him. Shaking his head, he thought it to be his imagination. Riding with the tantalizing Jayne at his back all night was sure to invoke sexual thoughts. He tried to calculate how long it would be before he could finish with a bath and go to her. The king interrupted his thoughts.

"And the other three?"

"I don't think they knew either. They seemed shocked by our ways. At the time we thought it nervousness from traveling to a new land, now I'm not so sure." He took another drink, trying to ignore the strange tingling all over his body. A flash of a soft breast covered with trailing soap filtered through his vision. Heat instantly surged through him, centering over his cock. He cleared his throat, coughing as he forced the image from his mind. "Lady Jayne said she woke up here with no clue as to how or why."

"But, you have explained it to her. She understands she must stay as your wife." The king's frowned deepened. "I do not want marital chaos in my kingdom, especially amongst my noblemen. We need this trade agreement to work. More brides mean more children. Within a generation we'll have more knights to defend this kingdom. Already the Caniba outnumber us by at least threefold. Then, who knows, maybe this war will end and we'll wipe the beastly scourge from existence. I should like to be remembered as the king whose actions started the downfall of our enemy."

"The decision was made," Ronen stated. This time it was a feminine hand pushing between narrow hips. Its direction unmistakable as a finger glided to the top arch of his wife's pussy. "I will make it work."

Ronen, come to me in the bath. I want you. Ronen grunted softly, mentally trying to lessen the pressure between his thighs as Jayne's voice filled his head. *I know you can hear me, my lord. I can feel that you do. My body is all wet for you.*

"Good, good." Wilhelm nodded.

Ronen, please...

"You are a man of great honor," the king continued.

Though hard to concentrate with images of his self-pleasuring wife in his head, he managed to focus enough on the conversation at hand to say, "But before there are more problems, methinks we should postpone trading with Divinity until the terms can be clarified. Sorin and I will find a way to convince our wives, and Sir Vidar is a good man, but if there are others who are not willing..."

Ronen! Mm, I feel so hot. The words were accompanied by the vision of Jayne's hand gliding between her thighs, long fingers disappearing between the soft folds of her sex only to come out wetter than before. *Why won't you come? I want to feel you inside me.*

"Chaos could ensue," the king finished. "It would not do to have a country of discontented wives. I will give this matter more thought."

Ronen, I'm about to explode.

"Oh, yea," he whispered, seeing her hand moving faster. Ronen rubbed his thumb over his fingertips. It was almost as if he could feel her against his flesh.

"My lord?" the king questioned, staring strangely at him.

"Um," Ronen coughed. By all the blood-covered battleaxes in Staria, his cock hurt and his balls ached. "Yea, a wise decision, Your Majesty. Very wise."

The king gave a small chuckle. "Well, my lord, it's the only kind I make. Now, let's have another drink."

Ah, Ronen, you're missing it. You'd better hurry or I will finish without you.

Ronen grunted in pain, before clearing his throat. "Yea, a drink."

✕

By all the gods of war!

Ronen tugged at his belt as he raced through the passageway leading to the guest chambers he shared with Jayne. Holding the belt tightly in his fist, he pressed his hand to the wall of a narrow stairwell as he took the steps three at a time. Why did the queen have to put them so far away from the main hall?

It had been nearly impossible to concentrate while the king talked. Images of Jayne's wet, naked flesh haunted him. After he managed to breathe past the increasingly painful press of his erection to his breeches, he realized she teased him on purpose. He could practically hear her giggling in his head.

Ronen pushed through the thick wood door without pause, grabbing the edge and slamming it shut behind him. Jayne stood in the bath, the light from the outside windows illuminating her from behind. She let him look, posing perfectly still.

The belt slipped from his fingers and he jerked his tunic over his head, throwing it aside. It felt great to have the dirty material off his skin. He walked toward her, kicking his boots off with more speed than grace. Jayne's arms lifted as she put her hand on her hip, turning slightly to the side. The light caressed her breast. Ronen nearly tripped over his own feet, unable to stare, walk and unlace the ties holding his breeches up at the same time.

"How was your meeting with the king?" Jayne laughed and he saw her body shake ever so slightly.

"That was a devilish game, my lady." Ronen finally freed his hips, pushing down the material. His cock only seemed to ache more now that it didn't have the pressure of his clothes to keep it down. "And now you will relieve the pains you've caused."

Eagerly, he climbed into the bath, splashing as his feet broke surface. The warm water lapped his calves. Without thought, he reached for her, pulling her clean, naked body hard against his chest.

Jayne threw back her head and chuckled. "Into the water, Ronen. You smell like your horse."

He growled in frustration. She was right, of course. Instead of letting her go, he forced her into the bathwater with him. A gentle current rushed by his knee as the tub filtered the mineral water. "And you smell like a wood nymph."

"I have no clue what that is." Jayne wrapped her arms around his neck, bringing him to her lips. "But I assume it's a compliment."

Ronen couldn't deny himself. He had to kiss her. His lips pressed hard against her mouth, staking fervent claim. She'd teased his libido to the point of breaking, made him feebleminded before the king, unable to concentrate. The driving need of his cock took over, telling his hands to spin her away from him, urging his hips to force her to the edge of the tub, making his hands reach under the water to spread her thighs from behind. He took his shaft in hand, guiding it like a sword into its sheath. The warmth of the blue mineral water heated his way, allowing him to glide into the sweet cavern of her sex.

Desperately, he thrust, groaning loudly to feel the tight muscles of her pussy gripping him. Friction and mineral water added an element of pleasure. The force between them became hot, enflaming his already warm cock. He couldn't stop, couldn't let go, though he desperately wanted to reach around to cup her breasts. But if he released her, their bodies might slide apart and he needed to finish too badly.

Ronen slammed into her, taking her rough and hard. The sound of flesh smacking flesh mixed with the splashing water. Jayne didn't protest. He wasn't sure what he'd do if she did.

And then, finally, blessed release. His balls tightened as he jerked to a stop. A harsh cry escaped his lips as he pumped his seed into her. For a moment, he held still, his heart hammering and his breathing ragged. Ronen's cock slid from inside her as he fell back into the tub, letting the warm water caress him like her pussy did his shaft.

Jayne turned and he expected to see a sated smile on her mouth. Instead, she grinned impishly. That's when he realized he hadn't felt her finish. He'd been so driven by her self-pleasuring torment, he'd gone temporarily mad.

"I will do right by you, my lady," he managed. A small fear wrapped around him. What if she discarded him as an inept lover? "You will find your pleasure many times this night."

"Once or twice will do," she laughed. "It's been a long couple of days and I'm exhausted."

"If you would not have run—"

"Don't, Ronen." She held up her hand. "Not today for there is no agreement to be made on the subject. It is in me to run and it is in you to capture."

Simple and matter of fact. Ronen sighed. "Very well, my lady. We will not discuss it now."

Jayne pushed up from the tub. She gestured to a door. "Why do all these castle bedchambers have two rooms in them like a his and hers suite at some fancy hotel?"

"I do not know what a hotel is, but all noble quarters have two chambers—one for the lady and one for the lord."

"Let me guess." She grabbed a drying linen from where it had been left on the bed and wrapped it around her body. "The ladies get stuck in the room with no outside door."

"Of course." Ronen took soap and began lathering his skin and hair.

"All wives are prisoners?"

"All wives are protected," he corrected. Why did she insist on seeing life with him as a prison? He would give her anything, all she had to do was ask. He'd slay an army for her, climb the northern mountains, give his own life to save hers. "Women need their own room so that husbands do not take too great advantage of the marriage bed. And I've been told there are rituals a lady performs that men are not allowed to see."

Jayne picked up a comb and began trailing it through her damp locks. He watched her from the corner of his eye, transfixed by the feminine scene. "What if I told you I wanted the room next to the main door?"

"I would know you wished to slip out in the middle of the night again." Ronen dipped under the water, rinsing the soap from his flesh.

"So it is a prison."

Ronen brushed his hands over his hair, wringing the water from the length. He sighed in exasperation. "It is necessary for protection, especially since we are so close to the borderlands here. If there were to be an attack, ladies would be the very last thing the Caniba creatures would find. It is for your safety."

✕

JAYNE SHIVERED, holding her bathing linen tighter as she watched Ronen step from the tub. Rivulets of water glided down his skin, running onto the stone floor. Thick, bulging muscles sculpted into the perfect specimen. From the tight cords of his neck to the defined lines of his stomach, the tapering of his hips and the strength of his thighs, she couldn't help but look. His penis lay nestled between his thighs, and she wanted to touch it and watch it grow.

She automatically grabbed the other thin towel and tossed it at him. Seeing his naked body teased her senses and her pussy already begged for more. She knew she'd tortured him to the brink of sanity with her images, pushing him to take her hard and fast. Though she enjoyed it, she hadn't met with the earth-shattering climax her body craved.

"Are all the Caniba like those who took me?" Jayne didn't want to think of the beastly men who'd had her tied to a pole.

"Yea."

To her disappointment, he wrapped the linen about his waist, hiding his lower half from view. "I guess I owe you thanks for freeing me. I should have said something at the time, but I..." She gestured weakly. "I don't do well with help."

"Then I guess I accept." The corner of his mouth twitched up.

"I've been to a lot of dimensions and dealt with a lot of dark characters, but there was something about those guys that froze my insides." Jayne shivered, remembering their eyes. Paige hadn't been lying. "They had dead gazes. I remember seeing that glassy look when I lived on the streets. All the residents of drug alley had that unaware sheen to them. The Caniba had the glassiness but with complete awareness. It's hard to explain. It's like a force drives them to act, but they're mindless at the same time."

"That force would be Sorceress Magda," Ronen said. Jayne lifted the comb, absently handing it to him to use. He turned his back to her as he walked to a trunk in the corner. She watched the muscles of his back swimming beneath the tight flesh. "She wields control over her followers like a goddess. Many believe her to be immortal."

"Do you?"

"Logically, I want to say no, but there are times..." He tossed the comb into the trunk and let the lid fall shut. Waving his hand in dismissal, he said, "You do not wish to hear of war."

She stiffened. "Why? Because I'm a woman? I'll have you know war doesn't bother me. I've seen more violence than—"

"I only meant that you wished for..." He grinned. "Was it to be finished two times?"

Jayne's breathing deepened. If her pussy could

scream in approval, it would have. Moisture flooded her sex, wetting the folds in welcome. "I'm pretty sure you said three."

"Did I?" He grinned.

"Perhaps four, five," she paused, biting her lip as she pretended to think. "No, it was fifteen that you said."

Ronen smiled even as he groaned. "You will be the death of me, but what a way to die."

Jayne laughed, unable to help herself.

"Remove the bathing linen and lie on the bed with your legs apart," he ordered, plucking at his waist. His towel slithered to the floor. "I wish to taste you and feel you come against my lips."

Jayne didn't try to resist as she dropped the towel and crawled onto the soft bed. Though she was in his possession once more, she assured herself nothing had changed. She'd find a way to leave him. Until then, she would enjoy her prison and manipulate her captor. Why should she deny herself something she wanted?

His fingers started at her foot, massaging slowly. Ronen's gaze focused on her, watching intently as he moved up her ankle to her calf. He explored her, taking in every inch of her legs, pausing to place random kisses to her flesh. Jayne closed her eyes to the pleasure, her mind focused on his touch.

A warm tongue darted along her inner thigh and she jerked, liking the way his breath cooled the wet trail he'd just made. She parted her lips, trembling in an effort not to force his head between her legs and smother him with her sex. Ronen nipped at her flesh, biting the tender crease where leg met pussy.

He groaned softly, the sound vibrating against her. She panted for breath, gripping the coverlet into tight fists. His mouth passed her center fire and moved over her hips, giving them the same attention he'd given her legs. He kissed her navel, swirling it with his tongue. He licked and bit over her stomach and ribs, massaged her sides, cupped her breasts but denied the hard nipples.

Before Jayne realized she'd let go of the covers, her hands were in his hair, urging his mouth to a taut nipple. It ached for stimulation, for the biting kisses he so generously gave the rest of her. Ronen chuckled, obeying her needy directions. He sucked the nipple hard, rolling it with his tongue.

Jayne parted her thighs wider, rubbing her legs along his hard flesh. She tried to grab his cock, but he turned his hip, denying her reach. So instead, she scratched at his waist, dragging her nails so they left red streaks in their wake.

"Ah," she gasped, pushing his head, "down."

The short plea was all she could manage.

Ronen chuckled, not moved by her strength as he took his time. Instead of obeying, he kissed his way to her neck, clearly not stopping until he'd touched and explored every inch of her.

"It is your turn to be teased, my devilish lady," he whispered before sucking the lobe of her ear.

Jayne became more aggressive, scratching at his arms and back, mindlessly trying to push him where she wanted him. Ronen resisted all her silent efforts as he made his leisurely way back down, reversing the path he'd first taken. Lips wrapped her nipples. His tongue flicked its way down her abdomen. Fingers gripped hips and ass.

"Please, Ronen." Jayne went from commanding to begging. There wasn't an inch of her flesh that didn't tingle, and she worried he'd make her turn over so he could journey up and down her backside. She couldn't take the torture if he did.

The bright light of late morning washed over them. To her relief, he merely ran his hands over her legs, not following with his slow moving mouth. Harsh breath hit against her sex, cooling and heating it at the same time. She felt the moisture gathered there, ready to ease his way.

Finally, he dipped his tongue into her folds, parting her sex as he tasted her. She grabbed his hair, doing her best to keep him there as she wrapped her legs around his shoulders. Ronen gave her pussy the same attention he'd given the rest of her. He probed her clit with his mouth until she cried out in sheer ecstasy. She watched the top of his head bob gently. Jayne squirmed, rocking into his mouth. He ran his hands up her stomach to rub her breasts. Her legs tightened, forcing him harder against her sex.

A sensual chuckle escaped him and he braced himself on the bed to push up. He inhaled deeply. "I will be no good to you passed out between your thighs."

Jayne was too close to completion. She moaned, tightening her grip to slam his face back into her sex. He bumped her clit and she jerked, nearly coming off the bed. Her leg slipped off his shoulder. She came hard, violently shuddering.

Her limbs sprawled on the mattress. She couldn't move and wasn't sure she wanted to. Ronen crawled next to her, grinning with pride as he lay on his side.

"You look proud." Jayne laughed weakly.

"That is one, my lady," Ronen answered. "Catch your breath, I owe you fourteen more."

Jayne rolled to face him, searching his face to see if he was serious. There was no way her body could take that another fourteen times in one evening. He merely smiled at her like a man who was very willing to try. She placed her hand on his neck, tracing his cheek with her thumb. "When did you shave?"

"On the horse last night while you slept. Soldiers learn to do what we can on the move."

"What else do you do on the move?" She continued to trace his cheek before moving to brush past his lips.

"We eat."

"Uh-huh." Jayne lazily swiped along the seam of his mouth when his lips closed.

Ronen nipped at her thumb, sucking it between his lips and biting gently. His lids lowered over his eyes. "We drink."

Now wet from his mouth, she again ran her finger around his lips. Her heart quickened. "And?"

"When we are alone, traveling those dark nights, we occasionally find our release." He turned his face into her palm, licking it. "And, when we are fortunate enough to have a woman, we fuck."

"While riding?"

"Yea, my lady."

Jayne furrowed her brow, trying to picture them doing such a thing.

As if reading her thoughts, he said, "Here, I will show you."

"You want to go for a ride now?" she inquired in disbelief. Jayne glanced at the lighted window. It still looked early in the day. Even so, she doubted she'd have the energy to make it out of the castle, let alone to the stables and onto a horse.

"No, my lady." He moved up on the bed so his upper back was pressed against the headboard. His cock was full and she realized whereas she had found release, he had not. He absently rubbed his stiff erection. "I wish for you to ride now."

Jayne licked her lips, eyeing his cock. "What if I don't want to ride? What if I'm hungry instead?" She lifted her leg, straddling his calves before leaning over. "What if I want to..."

Jayne flicked her tongue over the mushroomed tip, tracing the small indention she found there. His hips jerked and he reached over his head to grab hold of the headboard. She continued to tease him as he had her, flicking and licking, kissing and tasting. His legs worked against the bed, bumping up into her moistening pussy. Her breasts brushed along his muscled thighs until her own teasing began to torture her as well.

"Either take me fully into your mouth or mount up, my lady," he grunted. "For if you don't, I cannot promise to control my actions."

"Oh?" She sucked lightly on the tip, but only taking him as deep as the top ridge of his penis. Jayne wanted to ride him, but she also wanted to hear what else he had in mind. "What will you do when you lose control, warrior?"

"I will either grab you by the hair to forcibly fuck that temptress mouth of yours until I come down the back of your throat, or I will turn you around so that I may pound into you from behind like a wild beast in heat." The words came out harsh and panted, and he looked almost as if he didn't want to say them. "I have no desire to treat you so roughly and am ashamed I am so close to losing control."

Jayne had a very big desire for him to treat her so roughly. She crawled up onto his lap. Grabbing the headboard for support, she lifted up. Ronen grabbed her hips, as he maneuvered his cock along her slit. Quickly finding what he sought, he pulled her down onto him. A loud moan sounded over her as he buried himself deep.

Jayne lifted up and let her weight carry her back

down, keeping it slow and steady as she impaled herself on his cock. Ronen gripped her tight, digging his fingers into her flesh as he tried to make her go faster. His face buried between her breasts as he made animalistic noises along her flesh.

"This is my ride, Lord Ronen," Jayne said, nipping at his ear. He groaned, finally giving over all control. As a reward, Jayne moved faster, slamming onto him. The pleasure built and she had to throw back her head in order to catch her breath. She gasped and panted, both fighting and accepting the rush of tremors that overtook her body, radiating from her sex.

Stiffening, she couldn't move. She came hard. Ronen cried out, his stomach tensing as his hips jerked up. He spilled his seed inside her, not letting go of his tight hold on her until every last ounce of their climax was spent. Jayne's forehead fell against his shoulder.

"There are so many ways my mind wishes me to take you," he said into her hair. "But my body needs to recover."

Jayne suppressed a yawn, too spent to move. "Now that you mention it, I am a little tired. We might have to hold off on numbers three through fifteen until later."

"As my lady wishes." He kissed her temple as he rolled her onto her back. "Would you like me to carry you to your bed?"

He really was going to kick her out of his bed? Jayne stretched her arms over her head. It was just as well. She couldn't sleep on the soft mattress anyway. Closing her eyes, she yawned, not in any hurry to move. "No, I can do it."

When she made no move to get up, she felt his arms slip under her back and legs. Ronen lifted her, carrying her naked across the chamber to her room. She didn't open her eyes, too tired to demand he put her down.

"Rest you well, my lady," he said, laying her on a different but equally soft bed. His hand brushed over her hair before the sound of his footfall faded across the chamber floor.

The cool mattress was an odd contrast to her heated body as he let her go. Mumbling, she answered, "Goodnight, Ronen."

8

SHE DID IT AGAIN. She left him.

Ronen stared at Jayne's empty bed in disbelief. He'd awoken rested and ready to make good on his promise to give her pleasure. Almost eagerly he went to her chambers, hoping to slip into her bed and pull her from sleep with his kisses. But she wasn't there. The bed was made, untouched.

Outside, the telltale streaks of evening encroached upon the land. How long had she been gone? How did she sneak past him without rousing him? He was a trained knight. No one was supposed to enter his sleeping quarters without him knowing. Men could tiptoe across the dirt outside his tent and he would notice. But somehow his wife went right by him and he didn't know it.

She left him.

Ronen felt a panic rise inside him causing his hands to shake. How could she do it? Here? The same day Ronen assured the king he'd make his marriage work.

Maybe she didn't leave. Maybe she went below stairs and even now sat with the queen, dining and talking of the secret things women discussed.

Going to the trunk in his room, he found a loose tunic and breeches The soft linen material wasn't cut to fit him but, considering he didn't have his own clothes, he couldn't complain. He grabbed his boots, tugging them on before hurrying toward the main hall.

Be there, Jayne. Be in the main hall. Do not leave me.

He paused, hidden around the corner as he tried to center himself. His hands still shook and his heart pounded hard. Anxiety gripped him, tightening his chest and throat.

Be there, Jayne.

He strode into the hall, seeking the head table. Queen Patricia sat by herself, her hands folded in her lap, her chin lifted regally as she watched the hall. Occasionally, she would motion a silent command to a servant. Much of the evidence of the eve meal had been removed from the tables, but knights still sat, drinking and talking. King Wilhelm joined his men at a lower table, drawing his finger over the wood to illustrate his point. The knights around him laughed, pounding their fists on the tabletop.

Seeing Ronen, the king's expression dropped and he stood, leaving his companions to watch after him. When he was within speaking range, he said, "Is there news from the forest?"

"No, Majesty," Ronen answered. "It is my wife."

"Is she injured? Did the Caniba violate her?" The king took his arm, leading him to the privacy of the passageway beyond the main hall.

"Methinks she has run off again. I woke up and she was gone." Admitting as much pained him, but he would not dishonor himself more by lying to the king. "Has she been to the hall?"

"No," the king shook his head in denial. "The queen would have demanded her presence at the head table had she arrived."

"I will ask about the encampment and see if any have seen her pass. With your permission, I ride at once."

"Yea, in a moment." The king made a low noise of irritation. "You are right, Lord Ronen. If a bride of Firewall, with all its power and glory, cannot be convinced to stay, then we cannot risk others coming here under the present agreement. I will suspend trade with Divinity, but we will keep this between us. I have no wish to dampen the spirits of the men with Sorceress Magda threatening our borders. The knights need a reason to fight, and the hope of a lady always seems to be the best motivation. Moreover, I am not ready to give up on this alliance. I will not have the trade agreement tarnished by rumors of the gods being angered with us for trying to take more brides than they readily bestow."

"Agreed." Ronen itched to be dismissed so he could run for his horse. Hopefully someone in the encampment stopped her. Surely news of her first attempt to escape him had made the rounds amongst the men. Just the thought made him tense. The embarrassment to his honor was unbearable. First, she chose him for all to see, and then she ran from him—twice. Any way a man analyzed the situation, it looked bad for Ronen.

Then there was his private torment, the insecurities he'd never felt before. Ronen had no instinct as to how to deal with them. Show him a battle and his instinct was to fight. Show him a sword and his instinct was to swing. Show him a wife and his instinct was to make love to her and protect her from all harm. Jayne didn't want him to protect her.

Why did she run? He didn't mistreat her. He had money and power. She would never want for anything. What more could she want from him? Was facing the Caniba in the forest so much better than staying as his wife? What had he done? And the most humiliating question of all, was he a bad lover? The women in his past never complained, though he knew he wasn't as experienced as a man who'd been wed for several years. It's not like women lined every street yearning for a man to take them. When women of trade were available, he had to wait his turn like everyone else.

"When you find her, Lord Ronen, the queen would like to speak with Lady Jayne. She will ensure the new bride knows her place." The king motioned that Ronen should go.

As he hurried through the passageway, avoiding those gathered in the main hall, his irritation only deepened. Now the queen wished to interfere in his marriage?

Ronen's fists tightened and he fought the urge to scream. This was too much. It was beyond anything a knight of his station and training should have to deal with. Jayne embarrassed him in front of his king and his people. She humiliated him, tormented him and worried him. All he wanted was a wife he could take care of and do his duty by. He wanted ease in his home and happiness.

Why did the gods curse him?

✕

JAYNE STRETCHED her arms over her head and yawned. The fur pelt beneath her naked body tickled her flesh, padding it from the cool stone floor. She felt as if she'd slept for a year, glad for a bed that wasn't a pile of dirt beneath a shrub.

Grabbing the side of the bed, she pulled herself up from the floor. On the opposite side of the thick mattress, the door to Ronen's room was closed. The fire that burned when she walked into the room had died down to a soft glow. Combined with the darkened skies outside her windows, it made for heavy shadows. Jayne crossed to the fireplace and tossed in a log. The wood had been soaked in a sticky substance that instantly ignited but apparently caused the wood to burn slower and last longer.

Light crept brighter over the walls. The room was smaller than the one originally provided for her at Battlewar Castle. Two windows dominated one wall on either side of a thick chair. A small table, trunk and the box of firewood took up the other. The centerpiece of the room was the large bed whose thick mattress forced Jayne to sleep on the floor atop the fur rug.

A basin of water had been left on the small table and Jayne washed her hands. Next to it, she found a white, shapeless gown and a red corset top. A pair of short boots had been placed nearby on the floor. She'd seen how the women of this dimension dressed but refused to wear a corset tightened to the point she couldn't breathe for the sake of her cleavage. Before putting the clothes on, she tiptoed to the door leading to Ronen's room. He had promised to make her come, what was it? Fifteen times? Her rested body eagerly wanted to make good on the claim. Cracking open the door, she found the bedcovers messed up and the room empty.

She sighed in disappointment. So much for the idea of a quick romp before searching for food. Her stomach growled loudly. The maid who'd shown her to the guest chambers when they first arrived had offered to bring her food. Jayne should have said yes but, at the time, conceding she needed anything from Ronen or his people had been too much of a sting to her pride.

Slipping into her clothes, she left the corset loose and headed toward the passageways outside the chamber door. The castle was quiet. Each step sounded on the floor with a decisive hit. Jayne itched at her arm, pulling up her sleeve to check the wound. It had healed to a light pink, the skin only slightly textured.

The castle's layout was relatively simple compared to the maze of Battlewar. All passageways seemed to converge on one center spot—the main hall. Thick tapestries lined the walls, covering the stone with bright blues, reds and golds. They depicted bloody battles against legions of hairy Caniba warriors. From what she could decipher of the stories, they rarely ended happily for the hero.

Jayne understood fighting and the images didn't bother her as it might a more delicate lady. She might not go into battle, but each time she went into the ring she risked her life. Matches where death was a possibility paid more. Sure, she never actually killed someone in the ring, and the thought of killing for sport made her stomach curl, but she would if she had to. That's what some people didn't seem to get. Life wasn't some pretty day at the park, picnicking and laughing. Life was dirty and raw and filled with things she'd rather not think of. Jayne touched a tapestry, running her finger over a thick Starian hero marred with the horrors of war. The Starians seemed to have the concept down, though. Maybe she and Ronen were more alike than she first imagined.

What was she thinking? Ronen was her captor and every good prisoner knew there were only two options—live and die under the will of another or escape. It wasn't in her nature not to fight and, if she died, it would be her own doing.

"I must be delirious. I need food," she mumbled to herself, swatting aimlessly at the embroidered hero before walking toward a narrow patch of light coming from the direction of the main hall.

Though remnants of a crowd remained, giving evidence through scattered goblets and pitchers of liquor, the hall was nearly empty. A few servants cleared the remaining trenchers of mostly eaten food. Jayne's gaze swept over the hall, landing on a long table set high above the others on a stone platform. For a moment she thought the lady staring back at her was a statue. The woman didn't move, merely sitting with her chin imperially in the air and eyes narrowed in irritation.

"Lady Jayne, I presume," the woman said, coming slowly to her feet. Each movement was slow and steady. Her red gown and perfectly matched corset contrasted the drab color of the stone behind her and the muted brown and cream of her table-cloth. It set her apart from the hall. Her hair had been pulled up high on her head, piled in curls, and she wore a thick band of gold around the base of her throat. "You may approach."

Jayne arched a brow but stepped forward. It didn't take a genius to deduce that this was the queen. Only royalty would carry such a self-deserving, pompous look on their face. Stopping below the table, she stood, staring up as the other woman stared down.

"We are displeased with you," the queen said.

"Uh, thanks?" Jayne drawled, giving minimal effort to keep the dryness from her tone. She didn't think it possible, but the queen's face tightened even more.

"We would like an explanation." The woman walked very slowly around the table, not taking her eyes off the new "subject".

"We don't know what you're talking about," Jayne mocked. This woman didn't scare her. If Bossman Bishop and his goons couldn't make her throw a fight with intimidation, this slender thing hardly inspired alarm. Besides, Lady of Red here might be a queen, but she wasn't Jayne's queen—

despite the royal's supposed assumptions otherwise. The woman's lip curled slightly, and Jayne found some amusement in watching her try to retain her composure. As she stepped onto the lower floor, the queen made a wide arch around Jayne, studying her.

"Margaret," the queen ordered, "send someone to find Lord Ronen. Tell him I've taken his wife to my chambers. And tell Renell she is needed."

"Yea, Queen Patricia," the servant said, putting a trencher back down on the table. She curtsied before rushing out the door.

"Huh, I wouldn't have taken you for a Patricia," Jayne mumbled. Okay, so now she was just finding an excuse to be insolent. But really, the woman made it too easy. "You seem much too fun for such a serious name. How about we call you Patry? Or Trix?"

More like Prunella or Prudence. Jayne tried her best not to smirk. Hair of the smelly dog, she hated women like this! They were always so haughty and condescending. She bet the queen didn't know the first thing about taking care of herself.

"I do not like your tone." The words were low and hard.

"What happened to we? Did your other personality leave? Couldn't take your attitude either?"

"We is myself and my husband, King Wilhelm,

but I am sure he wouldn't appreciate how you speak to me." Patricia gave Jayne a displeased once-over with her eyes, before ordering, "Follow me."

"No." Jayne didn't move.

"Follow me,' the queen turned to stare Jayne down, "or I will have you paraded naked through the encampment below before being drawn and quartered. The knights have been a long time without an entertainment."

Jayne couldn't help herself, she smiled. Maybe this woman wasn't so bad after all.

"You don't believe me?" Patricia stiffened, appearing inches away from issuing the threat.

"No, I believe you," Jayne said, giving a small laugh. "Actually, I'm impressed. I have no idea what drawn and quartered means, but you made it sound very terrifying. Let me guess? You have an artist sew the event of my naked parade into a tapestry and lock me in my quarters?"

"You are tied to horses and your limbs pulled from your body."

That gave Jayne pause and she didn't relish the prospect. "So, your chamber is where, your, ah, queen?"

"Your Majesty will do," Patricia corrected. "This way."

Jayne followed the woman from the hall. When they were alone in the passageway, she said, "Uh, I feel I should tell you. I'm not really 'into' women. I mean, I'm flattered you'd like some alone time with me, but—"

"And if I was," the queen interrupted, "a disrespectful, unkempt, dishonorable woman who does not deserve the title of lady would be my last choice. In this dimension, women know how to look like women."

Jayne looked down the front of her dress and pulled at her corset, twisting the loose garment back into place. For some reason she couldn't explain, the words hurt. She knew she wasn't exactly the most feminine woman in all the dimensions, but in her world—the underground fighting world—she was Jayne "The Sweet" Hart, lady of boxing.

"Are you coming?" The queen's words broke into her thoughts and Jayne realized she'd stopped walking.

"What exactly are we doing?" Jayne asked. "If you just wanted to speak to me, we could have spoken in the hall."

"You might be accustomed to talking in front of gossiping servants, not caring about the uneducated impression you make upon others, but I know my place in society. With my station comes obligation and I take my honor and that of my husband very seriously."

Now I'm uneducated? Ouch. The queen really knows how to throw a punch.

The queen opened a door, leading the way into a room. The lavish bedchamber was clearly decorated for a woman. Delicate gold flowers embroidered the thick red curtains hanging over the bed and windows, matching the cushioned chairs. A small sword and an assortment of knives dominated one wall. Jayne closed the door, but stood near the doorway, not stepping too deeply into the luxurious chamber.

"It is apparent to me that you are a woman well used to control, and you gain that control by either fighting, arguing or acting contrary to expectations." The queen took a seat on one of the chairs, not once losing her solid composure. She gestured that Jayne should sit. "You ran from a Starian nobleman. Not just any nobleman but a brother of Firewall. You braved an unknown forest in an unknown land. You were kidnapped by the Caniba and kept yourself well. And, you stood up to me. Foolish, all these things, but brave."

Jayne sat but didn't relax. The queen appeared very reasonable, and she felt a little bad for her initial reaction to the woman in the hall. Patricia was right. Jayne's first instinct in any situation was to either antagonize or fight. It's what her childhood had trained her to do. When you lived in an orphanage or out on the streets, you learned to keep your emotions buried until they became habit to ignore.

"Did I leave anything out?"

"Only that Divinity more or less kidnapped me first and abandoned me here without my knowledge," Jayne answered. "Oh, and I was chased by a pack of wild boars."

"Lord Ronen spoke of Divinity to the king," Patricia acknowledged. "It is not in the Starian nature to rethink any decision once it's made. To do so negates the fact you made a decision in the first place. Indecisiveness is looked at as weak, and we are well used to making decisions at a moment's notice. But rest assured, we will be negotiating with Divinity again. They clearly do not understand the terms we set."

"Oh, I'm sure they understood," Jayne said. "The others that came with me didn't know what they were in for either."

"This is distressing information." The queen frowned. "Our ancestors would raid villages and claim the women they wanted with force. Centuries of war breeds such actions out of necessity, but we have progressed since then. The breeding ceremonies are an evolution of those raids, symbolizing the old ways and showing how we've changed as a people. But the women know why they are there and participate out of willingness or necessity—like those the gods send through the fairy rings. Like you, such women have no family or home in Staria and must seek protection."

"But I have a life off this dimension." Jayne felt a ray of hope. The queen appeared very astute. Maybe she would help her. "I have means to protect and take care of myself. I don't need or want a husband. All I want is an inter-dimensional jump home."

The queen nodded, but didn't speak.

"Will you help me?"

"You showed honor in coming back here after running a second time. That gives me hope," the queen answered.

A second time?

"So you will help me?" Jayne implored.

"Yea, I will help you." The queen paused and Jayne almost broke into a grin, only the next words stopped her. "I will help you adjust to your new station as Lord Ronen's wife and a noblewoman of Firewall."

"But..." Jayne jumped up from her chair. "You don't believe me?"

"I believe you," the queen said, not getting up from her chair, "but there is nothing to be done for it. You are Lord Ronen's bride. It is done and cannot be undone. All I can do is to ensure your situation does not happen to others in the future. We will speak to Divinity and try to come to a better arrangement. Unfortunately, women are a scarce resource and Divinity gives us what our men so desperately need."

"What if I dishonor my husband?" Jayne asked, feeling trapped and desperate. "What if I keep running? Or cheat on him? Or, or..."

"I think you bluff. You must feel something for him. You came back this second time, why?"

"Second time?" Jayne threw her hands into the air. Had the whole universe gone mad? "What are you talking about?"

"Lord Ronen searches the forest for you even now. I sent a man to bring him back so he could call off the search." A knock sounded on the door, light and fast. The queen stood to answer.

"But, why? I was sleeping in my chambers. Is he blind? I was right there on the floor in front of the fire."

Pausing at the door, Patricia gave a slight frown.

"The floor? Hm, this is unfortunate. If you didn't run, then Ronen's humiliation will be twofold. He will be seen as insecure in his marriage and rash in his actions. Perhaps we should say you ran and came back to him. The fact you tried to escape once is bad enough." Before Jayne could answer, the queen let in a servant. "Renell, attend to the lady's clothes and hair. We do not wish for her to look like she crawled from the forest. When you are finished, send for the seamstress so gowns may be fitted immediately for Lady Jayne. She will also need a lady's maid assigned to her. Pick one from the staff until the lady finds another more suited to her tastes."

"Yea, my queen." Renell, a short, squat redhead with pale skin and a smattering of freckles, curtsied.

"Lady Jayne, I look forward to helping you understand the Starian ways." The queen left Jayne and Renell alone.

"Ach, my lady, let's get a comb through that wild hair of yours. Come, sit, Renell will take good care of you."

9

Jayne felt strange, almost afraid to move. The tight corset, the same one she'd sworn never to wear like the other women, pulled against her ribs. She'd been poked, prodded, measured and pulled. Renell had called in a team of women to help her. They piled Jayne's hair on her head, much like the queen's. Margaret scrubbed her fingernails and toenails and shaped them into rounded tips. Another woman rubbed her shoulders and neck. Okay, so that last part of the pampering treatment wasn't too bad and almost made her forget someone poked annoyingly at her toes. And at least they fed her. She'd devoured an entire tray of fruits and bread.

"So if women are scarce, why do I see so many working in the castles?" Jayne inquired.

"It is an honored position granted to the women of knights, my lady," Margaret answered. "Residing in a castle we are more protected than the villages, and we receive word from or about our husbands sooner."

"Does anything here happen that has nothing to do with protection and war?" Jayne eyed each of them in turn, noting their somewhat confused expressions. "Didn't think so."

"The traveling markets come here more often, as well." Renell giggled.

"Wonderful," Jayne drawled. "Nothing we girls like better than shopping."

The sarcasm was lost on them as they nodded in excited agreement. Renell held out her hand. "I bought this pretty ring last time the silversmith came."

"Pretty," Jayne said, barely looking. The maids continued talking about the marketplace, of what they would buy and what they already had. She really didn't pay much mind to jewels—though she'd been given a few to wear as advertisement. That homeless woman had been ecstatic the day Jayne decided to clean cut some of her promotional clutter. It wasn't like Jayne Hart could be seen publicly selling the stuff.

"What do you think, my lady?" Margaret asked.

What had they been babbling on about? Jayne pulled at her tight bodice, about to mumble something incoherently when the door swung open, saving her. Ronen appeared, windblown and stiff with rage.

"My lord," the servants greeted, almost in unison. Their giggling instantly died with his appearance.

"Leave us," Ronen ordered. The women practically ran from the room, and he kicked the door shut behind them. "What do you have to say for yourself?"

Jayne lifted her bare foot. "That Margaret wasn't done with my toes. See, two left."

"I am not amused, Wife." His fists clenched at his sides. Was that supposed to scare her?

"Well, that's your problem, Knight." She mimicked his tone, knowing all the while it probably wasn't the best thing to do. Prudence was never one of her strengths. "You have only yourself to blame for running off to the forest and alarming the king's army. I was asleep in my chambers. In fact, it is I who should yell at you. I had to sit and listen to the queen lecture me about honor, duty and my lack of education. And what's worse, she is just as bad as the rest of you. She knows I don't belong here and yet she, with all her queenly powers, does nothing to right the wrong."

"Keep your voice down, Jayne," Ronen warned. "You do not speak of Queen Patricia in such a way. She has earned the respect of our people, risking her life in battle to save her husband. She even had this chamber built so that if the Caniba attacked, she would be the first lady to fight and fall, giving others time to escape in the tunnels."

"Don't get mad at me. You embarrassed yourself." She crossed her arms over her chest, only to become aware of how exposed her chest was. Her breasts pushed up, showcased by the fit of the corset and low cut of her gown. Ronen noticed, too. His eyes went to her breasts and stayed. Jayne tried to pull at the laces along her back to loosen the corset's hold. "I already told you, I was asleep when you went running off. Maybe don't act so rash next time."

Steely eyes darted back up to meet hers. His voice a little hoarse, but no less angry than before, he said, "I checked your bed. It was not slept in."

"That's because I don't sleep in beds. I don't like the softness. I was on the floor." Jayne became aware of how alone they were in the queen's room. Ronen captured her attention whenever he was around, and her pussy chose that moment to remind her of the promise he'd made to make her come again. Cream instantly pooled along her folds, slickening her sex.

His brow arched in disbelief. "No lady chooses the floor to a castle bed."

"I've been trying to tell you, I'm no lady." Giving up on loosening the corset, she placed her hands on her hips and faced him down. The statement wasn't a lie. At the moment, very unladylike thoughts were traveling through her mind, and all of them had to do with freeing Ronen's cock from his breeches and making him take her right there in the queen's chamber. Oh, how his sensible honor would rebel at the suggestion. Knowing he'd resist only made Jayne want to seduce him more. She liked the dangerous excitement of fucking him in such a forbidden place, of making him so crazy he forgot himself.

Suddenly, the tight corset's constriction became pleasurable. It pressed into her aching nipples, rubbing them with each rushed breath. His eyes drifted over her length to again land on her chest. "You look very much like a lady to me."

"That's because they dressed me up." Jayne lowered her voice to a sultry whisper. She batted her lashes, keeping her eyes wide. "You should see what is underneath."

Ronen opened his mouth but no sound came out.

Jayne trailed her hand over the back of a chair. She smiled innocently, inching away from him to round the side of the bed. He disappeared from view behind the bed curtain.

"Come, my lady."

Jayne smiled to herself, recognizing the barely contained passion in his words. *How quickly rage turns to lust, my lord.*

She appeared from behind the curtain, looking at him from over the large bed. "That is exactly what I plan to do, Lord Ronen." She licked her lips, moaning, "Come."

"I will take you back to our rooms."

Jayne pulled at her skirt, lifting only to let go as she crawled forward onto the bed. With her ass wiggling slightly in the air, she said, "But I want you to take me right here."

Ronen glanced around, as if they stood before a crowd of people. As his body shifted, she saw the unmistakable outline of his arousal poking at the material of his long tunic.

"Haven't you ever wanted to be bad?" She licked her lips, keeping them parted. "Naughty?"

"You should not be on the queen's bed," he insisted, reaching a hand to her as if he'd help her off.

Jayne maneuvered back, forcing him to lean forward over the mattress if he wanted to grab her.

"What's wrong, Ronen?" She pouted. "Don't you want me? Undo your laces and let me see. If you need help rising to the occasion, I'd be happy to lend you a hand, or a mouth."

Instead of coming onto the bed, he marched around to the other side. Jayne pulled at her skirt, baring the back of her thighs before he got there. She spread her legs, pressing her elbows into the bed and her pussy up into the air. Moaning, she demanded, "Take me, Ronen. I'm burning for you."

Just let him try to refuse me.

He made a strange noise, reaching for her as if he'd pull her from the bed, but he was powerless against her seduction. His hand slid over her thigh. Jayne grew heady with control.

"We should not be doing this here." Ronen tossed her skirt up, baring her ass. Jayne heard the rustling of material behind her. When she glanced over her shoulder, she saw him tugging frantically at his breeches. His cock protruded, already tall and eager.

"You think too much about the rules." She gripped the covers, wrinkling the pristine bed.

"I think too much about you." Ronen jerked her hips, forcing her back. Her chest dipped as her arms slid out from under her, angling her body even more. His cock brushed across her ass. "I cannot get you out of my head."

Though sweet, she knew the sentiment only reflected the connection they shared. She was, literally, in his head as he was in hers. Jayne couldn't stop thinking of him. She knew the reason, but still found the fact disconcerting.

Her body heated, each nerve tingling with need. Her pussy felt so wet and desperate. The thick cock head probed her sex, gliding along her slit before finding its target as he stood beside the bed. Some of her control slipped but she didn't care. How could she? Now, in this moment?

The soft covers slid beneath her arms, as she tried to push back onto her elbows. Warm hands massaged her legs, holding her where he wanted her. Her heart quickened, seeming to pound violently in protest of the corset. She inhaled deeply, already breathless. Everything about the man intoxicated her.

Then he thrust, adding to the bittersweet torment brewing inside her sex. She gasped, her pussy stretching to accommodate him. Jayne squirmed, needing him to take her hard. The rich, lush chamber danced before her as she bobbed back and forth on the bed. She had full view of the door and she watched it in excitement, her ears straining past her lover's hard pants for a sign of an intruder.

Ronen drove forward, giving her what she wanted. She closed her eyes, feeling the size of him as he moved within her, pounding, plunging, faster and harder with each stab of his cock. Desperation surrounded them—to meet release, to finish before getting caught.

Jayne bit her lip, fighting the effort not to moan as release hit her. Her pussy quivered, gripping his cock in the primal effort to make him join her. Ronen buried himself deep and shuddered. He let loose a low groan, his hold on her weakening as he shook under the force of his climax.

Ronen's hands landed on the bed on either side of her body as he leaned over her backside. Gravity pulled her skirt over her ass. Jayne gave a small laugh, feeling powerful once more. He'd given in to her desires, going against everything to have sex with her.

"We should go." He breathed hard.

Jayne didn't deny it. She loved the thrill, but she didn't want to get caught. Half the fun of sneaking a quick bout in secret places was getting away with it. "Help me straighten the bed."

Jayne crawled forward, going to the other side. They pulled the covers straight, hiding all evidence of their lovemaking. Ronen's gaze met hers and he gave her a sated half smile. It would appear she'd discovered the way to cool his anger, and she made a mental note to remember it in the future. Ronen might be one of the most worthy opponents she had ever gone up against, but in the end she would win this battle. She would have her freedom.

✕

RONEN HAD no idea what had come over him. Well, that was a lie. He had an idea, and it was a sexy, dark-haired vixen who made his blood boil and his fists clench.

When she crawled onto the bed and swayed her ass in invitation, how could he refuse? And even though he wasn't sure he believed her when she claimed to be sleeping on the floor, he couldn't deny her physically. Jayne had a control over him that he didn't understand.

Ronen felt the eyes of the main hall on them as he led Jayne through, intent on taking her back to their room. The knights had returned to their drinking after being interrupted to search for a lady who wasn't actually missing. The queen gently spread rumors through her servants that Lady Jayne ran away but had a change of heart and came back, the pull of her handsome husband too strong. By the time Patricia finished dropping clues, most would believe running to be a cultural custom from Jayne's homeland to entice her mate. Ronen hated lying, but he couldn't naysay the queen in front of the castle so he kept his mouth shut.

Jayne suddenly turned toward the lower tables, sliding into an empty seat. Smiling at the couple of knights who sat there, she reached for their pitcher of mead and poured herself a goblet. Ronen watched, unsure if she would merely take her drink and continue on with him. When she didn't, he slowly sat across from her, aware of the awkward glances the men gave him.

"I saw you fighting out by the tents, didn't I? You have a killer left hook." Jayne motioned to Dersly's scarred left hand before giving a small punch through the air to indicate what she talked about.

Dersly followed her gaze, examining his hand as if he'd never seen it before. The big warrior grunted softly.

"My lady?" Ronen tried to stand, hoping to

prompt her to do the same. "Perhaps we should retire."

"I'm not tired. I slept most of the day," she answered. If he didn't already know her so well, he would have believed that look of innocence on her face.

Ronen frowned, not wanting to pursue the conversation and draw attention to the fact he'd sent the king's army into the forest to find a woman who might not have been missing to begin with. He lowered himself down once more, tensing with dread of what might happen next. He remembered all too well the way his brother's first wife flirted with the men of the castle.

"I bet you knocked out a few teeth in your time, too." Jayne lifted her cup to Gerald. Compared to Dersly's vast fighting experience, Gerald was an untried youth.

"My lady," Gerald nodded in affirmation, not as hesitant to return the lady's smile. "A fair few."

Jayne laid her hand out on the table. "I once hit a guy so hard his tooth became lodged between my knuckles," she paused, pointing at her hand, "right there. Let me tell you, Handsome Larry Turner wasn't so handsome after that."

It wasn't exactly what she said, but the animated

way in which she said it. Suddenly, the stoic Dersly laughed. The deep brusque sound echoed over the hall. Ronen could barely believe it.

"My lady likes to tell tales, Dersly," Gerald said, chuckling and nodding, and he took a long drink.

"It's the truth!" Jayne gasped in unconvincing affront. "I never lie about a fight."

"A delicate thing like you," Dersly managed in between laughing gasps of air, "hitting…" He pounded the table, unable to finish.

"You have no scars, my lady," Gerald said, as if that explained away her claim.

"I don't get scars," Jayne answered.

"Was he a wee man?" Dersly grabbed his stomach.

Ronen watched the scene unfolding before him in amazement. In the course of two seconds, Jayne had integrated herself with the knights. Watching her closely, he said, "It is the truth. I have seen for myself how she heals."

Knights began to gather around them, moving from across the room to hear what made the mighty Dersly so amused. As Gerald explained what happened, Jayne slapped her hands together.

"So, Dersly, you don't think I can hit a big man

like you?" Jayne kept her face composed, the almost innocent half smile on her lips.

"I welcome you to try, my lady." Dersly stood. "And I offer my face to the cause."

Laughter grew around the hall and fists began to pound in a steady, encouraging rhythm.

"Lady Jayne," Ronen began, intent on stopping her. The rambunctious noise surrounding them drowned out his reasoning.

"It hardly seems fair to hit a still target, but your face it is!" Jayne yelled, slamming her goblet down. The knights only cheered louder. She pushed up from the table and made her way to Dersly. Ronen didn't worry about the man. Not a one of them would dare hit the Lady Jayne. Besides, she had claimed to be a fighter. Leaning forward, he silently admitted to being a little curious as to what his wife could do.

Dersly still chuckled as he turned his face. Jayne lifted her balled fists, keeping her arms tight to her body. As fast as a striking serpent, her fist struck, hitting the knight square on the jaw. The cheering instantly died into a palpable silence. Dersly's head snapped back and he swayed slightly before righting himself. Then, very slowly, he reached to touch his face, rubbing the wound.

"This one isn't a lady, she's a warrior in a lady's

form," Dersly announced. "Methinks she could knock a man's tooth from his head."

The cheering erupted again.

"She hits harder than you, Gerald, to be sure," Dersly teased, inciting more laughter. "Bring the Lady Warrior of Firewall a drink. Let's see if she can hold her liquor like she holds her fist. Tonight, she celebrates like a true Starian knight!"

Finally, Jayne turned her gaze to him. She grinned, looking very pleased with herself, as if some strange plan she'd set into motion had come to fruition.

"A toast," Gerald called out, "to the Lady Warrior!"

Ronen had no choice but to grab his goblet as the men continued to cheer his wife. "To the Lady Warrior."

"I SAID I COULD FIGHT, but I never said I could drink," Jayne mumbled, swaying into Ronen's side as he helped her to their chambers. "Good think, thing, think, drink..."

His wife was drunk. No, she had ridden well past

the border of drunk and into the oblivion of nonsense.

"Good think I have the nanos. I would not want to feel my head tomorrow without them." Jayne giggled and draped her arm around his shoulders. She leaned her head onto his shoulder. Her breath a whisper against his neck, she said, "Mission accomplished."

"Mission?" Ronen stiffened and stopped walking. When he looked at her, she had closed her eyes.

"Mm, are we there?" Jayne asked.

He bumped her with his arm. "What mission, Jayne?"

Her lashes fluttered over her beautiful eyes. "What? Why are you glaring at me? You are the one who seemed all worried about what those men would think about me running away a second time, or not running away but you thinking I ran away. It's not my fault you didn't look on the floor. I hate soft beds, they're too soft."

He tried to take a step, but her feet didn't move with him. Sighing, he swept her up into his arms. Jayne gave a light moan and wrapped her arms around his neck.

"You were worried. The queen was worried. Margaret was worried. Renell was...well, Renell was chatty." Jayne moved in his arms, pressing her body against his chest. "You smell nice."

Ronen walked faster. Her lips brushed his neck, sending chills over his body.

"So I took care of it." Her hair tickled his chin. "I gave the knights something more entertaining to talk about."

"I don't think the queen would approve of your actions." Ronen had seen Queen Patricia pass by the hall. She had been far from pleased.

"I don't care. I much prefer the company of fighters. Men are easy, especially warrior types. Make a few jokes about fighting, prove you know what you're talking about by manipulating the biggest guy in the room into baiting you, take a punch or two with a smile and they'll let you glide right into their ranks. So much easier than dealing with women." She snorted. "Though I am kind of glad Dersly didn't hit me. He has really big fists."

"None of the men would dare to touch you." Ronen held her tighter, realizing there was a lot he didn't know about his wife. Just by watching her tonight with the others, he knew she was smart. She read people and fed off their reactions.

"That's not true."

Ronen stopped, tightening his grip as he got ready to turn back.

"Fredrick slapped me on the back and made mead go up my nose. It burned bad."

Ronen relaxed. Fredrick had been slapped himself and was knocked into Jayne.

"By the looks of the women around here, they are not the fighting kind. Now, when news spreads about me, I will be called Lady Warrior not Lady Runs-a-lot. And the men will speak of how I hit Dersly and held my liquor." Jayne moaned. "Well, almost held my liquor."

Ronen didn't want to tell her that after the first cupful, he'd ordered the servants to water hers down in secret. The mead had been strong and Jayne too slender. If he hadn't, she would have dropped dead on him.

"Mm, you feel nice. I love your hands. They're so strong." She wiggled again and he realized he'd begun massaging her as he carried her, kneading his hands on her thigh and near her breast. Jayne bit his ear. "Stop walking. Let's have sex right here."

"In the hall? But someone could walk by."

"It's late. No one is about." She bit harder, instantly licking the wound. "Come on, take me against the wall." Her hand glided up his arm. "You're so strong. I know you can lift me."

"You are far into your cups, my lady." He tried to reason, but it was hard to hold onto sanity when her breathy whisper begged him. "I will not take advantage of you."

"Why?" She chuckled. "I would take advantage of you if our roles were reversed."

His cock lurched to attention, very willing to be taken advantage of. Ronen's brain tried to resist.

"It will be quick, I promise." Her kisses hit his throat and hair, wherever her mouth could reach while he held her. "Just unlace your pants. I'll lift my skirt." She groaned into him, dragging her tongue over flesh. "Please, Ronen, I'm already wet for you. Put me down and take me against the wall."

"We're almost to our chambers." His words were hoarse and he walked faster. Having sex in such a place wasn't unheard of, but usually not where the queen resided. She had strict rules when she was in residence.

"No, here," she pouted. "Now."

Ronen couldn't take it any longer. His cock ached for the slick warmth of her body. How could he resist? His wife begged for him to take her and he wished for nothing more.

Ronen lowered her and she backed up against the wall, stumbling slightly. He eagerly reached to untie his laces, his fingers feeling thick in his urgency. Jayne pulled at her skirt in invitation. Finally managing to push his breeches from his hips, he went to her, crushing her against the wall.

Jayne gripped his shoulders, running a leg up his hip. Ronen pushed her up the wall, holding her thighs. Bracing her against the wall, he mindlessly pushed forward. The soft heat of her sex greeted the tip of his cock, enveloping it.

"Take me," she ordered, squirming.

Ronen plunged deep, enjoying the way her pussy clung to him. He ground his hips, rocking within her. Her cleavage bobbed with each push of his body, causing the tops of her breasts to dance erotically for his pleasure. "You will be the death of me."

"Ah," she gasped as he thrust harder. "No, I have no intentions of killing you."

"Just of leaving me." He quickened his pace, ramming into her as if he could make her want to be with him forever. Emotions warred inside him—fear that she'd leave him, the desire to hold her like this forever, anticipation of what she'd do next. Life with Jayne would never be boring.

Her sex began to quiver along his shaft. She dug

her fingers into his muscles, squeezing tight. Suddenly, she made a weak noise of release, her pussy engulfing him in jerking waves. Ronen thrust a few more times before meeting his own climax. He kept her pinned to the wall, his cock deep inside her.

"You don't have to go, Jayne. I will be good to you. I promise." He smoothed back her hair and her foot fell to the floor without his support. His shaft pulled free.

"I can't stay. This world isn't for me." She closed her eyes, refusing to look at him.

"How can you believe that? It's a war filled with fighters. You said it yourself, you understand our ways."

"Ronen, don't." She shook her head. "I'm not a wife. I can't give you a family."

"I have given the matter thought and we can help raise my brother's future children. They are blood and will be like our own. Or there are plenty of boys who have lost their parents. They need good homes."

"Orphans?" Jayne finally looked at him, her eyes glassy. "I can't take care of children, Ronen. All I want is to be free to travel the dimensions and to live on my own terms. Alone." Her head fell forward and she sighed. "I'm so tired. I don't want to talk anymore."

Ronen stepped from her just enough to grab his breeches and tug them up his hips. He tried to force her words from his mind, hoping that by not thinking about it, the pain inside his chest wouldn't hurt so much. Not bothering to pull the laces tight, he lifted her into his arms once more and carried her to her own bed.

10

"BLOODY FUCKING MISERY." Jayne's back felt as if someone stabbed her repeatedly along her spine. Moaning, she tried to move, managing to make it to her side to stare at the stone wall. She was all too aware of the fluffy softness surrounding her limbs. Why in all the dimensions was she in a bed? Naked?

She recalled hitting Dersly and bracing herself for a return punch before the man broke into laughter. The drinking she remembered. Singing drunken war ballads at the top of her lungs with a room full of inebriated knights was a little fuzzier.

Behind her a door creaked, but she didn't turn to see who it was. She must have spent the whole night in the same, unmoving position. Now her neck paid the price. Jayne groaned.

"Are you feeling the effects of drink?" Ronen inquired, as the bed subtly shifted.

"No. My head is fine." She groaned again as his weight jiggled her.

"See, the bed is not so bad, is it?" A warm hand slid along the small of her back and she focused on that heat. "The queen demands the best where she stays."

"Yes, it is bad. Horrible," she pouted. Jayne still didn't move, not even to squirm when he withdrew his hand. "It's like I have been thrown into the pits of hell and tiny demons with sharp feet are running up and down my spine."

"You did not mind it so much last night." Ronen kissed her neck.

"So, in the passageway? That was real?" Jayne summoned the cloudy memory, but only got vague impressions.

"Yea, my lady, very real."

"And the singing in the main hall?"

He chuckled. "Yea, my lady, you were very robust."

Desire stirred within her, making her forget her sore back. "And my taking you into my mouth against your chamber door?" Jayne licked her lips, confident she could remember the taste of him as he came into her mouth.

"Yea, my lady, you were very insistent." He began to massage her spine, rubbing his thumb in hard circles to loosen the knotted muscles.

"What about you bending me over the side of your bed? I have a vague memory of that." Jayne closed her eyes. Ronen's body gravitated closer and she thought to have felt the brush of his cock against her ass. Apparently, Ronen had a few ideas when he came to her room that morning.

Jayne glanced over the wall. Was it morning? The light shining from outside did appear bright.

"Yea, my lady." He kissed her shoulder and his erection grew bolder along her cleft. His heat radiated around her from behind, as he drew her to his chest. He pressed his body along her back, his hands skating up her body to cup her breasts. Ronen rubbed them gently and moaned. The naked, hard length of his desire for her was unmistakable. Licking her neck from pulse to earlobe, he whispered, "And once you held me down and rode me like I was a wild stallion you were trying to break. By the time you finished with me, methought you had drained my serpent dry." He rocked into her, causing her to instinctively arch.

Fingers ran down her stomach, holding her flush against him so she couldn't wiggle away. "But it would seem I am eager to be tamed by you once more."

Pleasure coursed through her. He pressed his hand lower while nudging his leg from behind. He parted her with his thigh, holding her legs open so he could explore the naked line of her moistening sex.

"So sweet," he murmured, his words vibrating against her.

Jayne gasped as his finger grazed over her clit. "What about that thing where you poured wine all over my feet and sucked on my toes for an hour?"

"I..." Ronen pulled back. His hands slid from between her legs, leaving her pussy aching desperately. "I did not do that."

She pressed her lips tightly together to keep from laughing. "Are you positive?"

"I did not drink and had my wits about me," he assured her. Then, sounding unsure as if he should be angry, he began, "Did someone—"

Jayne couldn't hold her amusement. Laughter escaped her. "Huh, it must have been a dream."

He relaxed some. "You wish for me to dine on your toes?"

"No, my lord." She turned around to face him, running the back of her hand over his thick chest.

Jayne loved touching his flesh, tracing his scars and exploring the muscular valleys. "I wish for you to not be so serious."

"If I am serious, it is your doing." He brushed the tip of his nose to hers. "If you would but promise to stay as my wife, I could relax."

Jayne couldn't meet his gaze, even though it was so close. A part of her actually considered what he offered until the logical part of her brain reminded her that the only thing she'd ever really, desperately wanted since those years in the orphanage was her freedom. How could she give that up now for a tight ass and delicious sex? What would happen when the flames between them died and they grew bored? The longer she stayed, the harder it would be to go. Already she found herself thinking positively about Staria and its people. She liked the knights, with their gruff, fighter ways and easygoing banter. She didn't care much for the clothes, but they could always be changed so it wasn't a big issue. The castle food tasted better than some of the finer dimensions she'd stayed in. Then there was Ronen—sexy, beautiful, masculine Ronen. Just thinking his name sent a shiver over her.

She looked at his chin, seeing the roughened texture of his whiskers sprinkling over his flesh.

Instantly changing the suddenly uncomfortable subject, she grabbed his cock and squeezed along the base. With a firm pull from root to tip, she felt it rise even more in her hand. Mimicking the slight accent of his people, she said, "Methinks there be other ways to relax you Lord Ronen."

At her touch, his lids drifted lazily over his eyes. "You twist my head, Lady Jayne, until I cannot think. You fight me, but then touch me like this."

"Trust me, for what I have in mind, you don't really need to think." Jayne pushed him so he rolled onto his back. Ronen's arms sprawled to his sides.

Jayne crawled on top of him, holding his strong body down with her smaller one. Her muscles twinged, but she ignored the pain. Leaning into him, she nuzzled her face against his rough cheek. Her nipples brushed across his chest, already hard from when he massaged them, and her pussy slid along his hard stomach.

Ronen moaned softly. "You are so beautiful. I could look at you forever."

Jayne gave a small laugh. "Forever's a long time."

Ronen pushed up from the bed, causing her to slide back onto his lap. His hard cock pressed against her ass as she became seated on his lap. "Stop."

"Stop?" Jayne's mouth fell open in shock before

she could hide the expression behind an uncaring mask. The truth was she found she cared very much. Stop? He wanted her to stop?

"Stop forestalling a true conversation." Ronen's hands braced his weight, but his eyes pierced into hers, holding her captive more effectively than any hands could. "If I try to speak of something real, you dismiss it or you start kissing me so I forget what I wish to say."

Jayne didn't move. How could she? His irritation washed over her. Instinct told her to do one of two things, seduce him or fight with him. Naked on a bed, his cock pressed intimately against her cleft, she didn't really feel like fighting him. And his expression forbade any attempt at seduction.

"You have nothing to say, do you?" He frowned, though a deep vulnerability shone through his gaze.

Jayne opened her mouth, but nothing came out. A real conversation? That wasn't necessarily fair. They'd had real conversations. She'd told him some about her past. He spoke of his homeland, duty and family. Even as she tried to rationalize, she knew what he meant. She refused to talk about them, their situation. Sure, she'd dismiss or ignore any attempt he made at convincing her to stay. A deep realization hit her. The reason she refused to discuss it was because she was terrified he'd succeed.

"Methought not." The moment passed with his flat words and hardening eyes.

"I don't know what you want from me," she whispered.

"Then I suppose what I want is not there for you to give." Ronen rolled her roughly onto her back. "I will have to settle for giving you what you want."

His kiss ground at her mouth, as if he would punish her. Jayne resisted for a brief moment, before the passion in him drugged her senses. She grabbed his hair, accepting his forceful handling, not minding the hard grip of his roaming hands or the bite of his teeth.

Their lovemaking became a battle. Hands gripped, nails raked, lips fought and bodies rolled. Jayne forced him over, reaching between her legs to grab his cock. She squeezed and Ronen grunted. Before she could impale her body on his, he had her on her back once more. His strong thighs forced hers apart. Her body buzzed with sensations. What had started as punishment turned into a mutual, frantic desperation.

Ronen grabbed her legs, lifting them over his shoulders, using her own body to keep distance between them. "Is this what you want from me? A hard cock?" he demanded, as if punishing her with the physical pleasure he offered.

Sweat beaded their flesh. As he drew his erection along her wet slit, she bucked off the bed. His hands braced next to her shoulders while hers roamed aimlessly over his chest—pinching nipples and scratching pinkened trails.

Ronen propelled his hips forward, sinking deep inside her willing body only to pull back out. The position allowed him to go deeper and rougher than ever before. Jayne met his hard rhythm, punctuating each slam of their bodies with an audible gasp for air, only to be outdone by his louder grunts. He didn't go slow or easy, instead plunging in and out at a wild pace.

"Ronen," she panted, clawing at his neck and shoulders. He kept his gaze steadily on her, forcing her to look at him. His eyes seemed almost chilled, having lost the soft light they normally carried when they made love. She hated the coldness in them, but couldn't look away, couldn't think of how to ask for the softer Ronen back. She'd pushed for this with her words and deeds and fears. Even as her body enjoyed the rough coupling, her heart revolted.

She began to tense, but he did not slow his pace.

Bittersweet pleasure erupted along her body. Her pussy tried to cling to him as she found release. Ronen thrust several more times, taking longer to find his end. Then, suddenly, he stopped, his hips flush against her. He growled, loud and long, screaming the gruff sound into the chamber. As soon as he finished, he rolled off her.

Sated and somewhat stunned, Jayne let her legs fall onto the bed. He breathed hard, not moving to pull her into his arms as he lay beside her. Gone was the considerate lover, replaced by the hard warrior who had just fucked her.

Before Ronen, sex had just been sex—a means to find selfish, momentary pleasure and nothing more. She hadn't realized just how different Ronen was, how tender and thoughtful he could be until he took that part of himself away. Now, as he took all emotion out of sex, she became all too aware of what she was losing. With Ronen, there had always been an intensity, uncalculated, unplanned, just there. But how did she get something like that back?

Jayne made no move to touch him, even though her fingers twitched and her hand lifted. She glanced at him but had to look away. She hated the cold chill in his eyes, despised herself for forcing it to be there. Maybe she wasn't meant to be loved or cared for. She wasn't any good at expressing such emotions, let alone asking for them from someone else.

Jayne opened her mouth, willing words to come out. She didn't know what they would be or what they would mean. But then he spoke, stopping her from trying.

"The king sent men to scout the borderlands," he said. "I'm going to ride out and join them. If I leave soon, I should be able to find them before they spread out."

Jayne didn't say anything, though questions formed inside her head begging to be asked. *You're leaving me? When will you be back? What if I try to run again? Do you even care? Why won't my voice work?*

Jayne frowned. She should be happy that he left her alone at the castle. Only now where would she run to? The Caniba had been a mistake. The portal wasn't anywhere to be found. But escape was what she wanted, wasn't it? Especially now after what sex with him had been reduced to. Could she really have a purely sexual relationship after she'd seen more from him?

Ronen rolled out of bed, striding naked across the room. She watched him, unsure what she should say or do, or of what she even wanted.

Stopping at the door, he refused to look at her as he said quietly, "My people do not put much faith in loving a woman, Jayne. It goes against everything it takes to be a hardened warrior. But what I feel for you has to be as close to that emotion as any knight of Staria can get."

Jayne didn't move, didn't act or speak. She lay stunned as he walked out of the chamber. Tears sprang into her eyes and a red-hot panic washed over every inch of her being. Instinct yelled for her to run away from any tenderness, said that it didn't matter if she ran to the Caniba or to live in the forest or to some unknown destination way beyond Ronen's reach.

Run, Jayne. Freedom.

Without thought, she jerked into her clothing, not caring that the blue corset with black laces didn't exactly match the red of the gown. She placed a strip of cloth between her teeth and brushed her hair away from her face with her fingers as she walked toward the door. Pausing before opening it, she tied her hair at her nape so the locks fell long down her back.

Touching the knob, she stopped. She heard Ronen on the other side. Her eyes swept over the chamber, knowing before she even looked there was no way out. The stone was too thick and if the windows opened, she didn't know how.

Trapped.

"What I feel for you has to be as close to that emotion as any knight of Staria can get."

Run, Jayne. Run far.

"Why did you have to say that? You could have said anything but that." She backed away from the door, bumping into the corner of the bed. Jayne didn't stop until she reached the far corner. Sliding onto the floor, she pulled her knees into her chest and hugged them tight. A tear slid over her cheek. "Goodbye, Ronen. I'm sorry. Now I really can't stay with you. Trust me when I say it is for the best."

RONEN TOOK a long time getting dressed, partly because his hands shook and partly because he watched the bedchamber door in hopes that Jayne would burst through and say something—anything— to him. He waited and she didn't.

What possessed him to speak those words? Had he really expected to be met with anything but the silence she'd given him? Jayne made her position very clear. She wanted nothing to do with him beyond what his body could give.

Ronen paused on his way out the door, giving her one last chance to come after him. If only she'd ask him not to go to the borderlands, to stay with her for whatever reason she chose to present. If only she would give him a glimmer of hope that what he felt wouldn't always be one-sided.

The woman twisted him up inside, made him feel things he never imagined possible. She toyed with his mind, dominated his thoughts and drove his body wild. Ronen had fought many foes in his life, but none so defeating as his fighting Lady Jayne.

"So be it," he said to himself, doing his best to steel his nerves as he marched from their shared rooms.

$$\times$$

GUARDS? He left her with guards?

Jayne frowned, staring at the two men standing outside Ronen's chamber door. They blocked her from leaving as she tried to make her way to the hall to get something to eat before exploring her options for escape from within the castle. Recognizing them as a couple of her singing companions from the night before, she forced a fake smile. "Why hello there, boys. Come to take a lady to lunch?"

The knights shared confused glances.

"To break my fast in the main hall," she explained, wondering why they didn't smile at her.

"Our orders are to escort you to the queen's chambers," Sir Harol answered. "This way, my lady."

"What if I order you, as a lady, to let me do what I want?" She batted her lashes and Harol looked as if he might waver.

"You do not have the authority to supersede our orders, my lady," the stoic Richard explained.

"Even if I promise to go to the queen's chambers after I eat?" Jayne kept her attention on Harol, the younger and more malleable of the two.

"We will see that a tray is brought to the queen's chambers for my lady." Richard motioned that she was to walk. Jayne stepped in front of him, feeling more like a prisoner than a guest.

"Did Ronen send you to guard me while he's gone?" Jayne asked. Even though the fact annoyed her, it also gave her a small sense of pleasure to know he cared enough to try to hold onto her.

"Turn right," Harol said.

Instead, Jayne walked straight into the main hall. Several of the tables were filled with knights. A couple bent over papers, drawing their fingers across maps. Others sat in deep conversation, slapping their hands to make a point. At her entrance, they turned to her and nodded in greeting. Jayne smiled back, unable to help herself.

"My lady," Richard insisted.

"What are you going to do?" Jayne arched a brow, shooting him with her most withering look. "Carry me?"

"If I must," he blustered.

Jayne laughed. She'd like to see him try. Noticing Dersly, she called to the man, "If you get these two sons of a whoring cat off my back, I'll owe you one!"

Dersly chuckled, but shook his head in denial. "Methinks my lady can handle her own cats well enough."

"Some champion you are," she teased, before sighing heavily. "Very well then, at least throw me the bread before they march me away."

Dersly obeyed, grabbing a loaf from the basket next to him and tossing in her direction. Jayne caught it and lifted it up in thanks.

"My lady," Richard insisted.

"Quit crowding me," Jayne warned him, growing more and more annoyed with each passing second. The pleasure she felt in Ronen caring about her staying soon faded into irritation at her personal guards' doggedness. "I'll go, but I'm walking at my own pace."

She took a deliberate bite of her bread, ripping it from her mouth. A few of the watching knights chuckled. Richard said nothing, but his face tightened in irritation. Harol tried to hide his smirk and failed.

"Well then, let's get moving," she ordered playfully, leading the way to the queen's chambers. "That way you boys can be on your merry ways."

"You are our merry way, my lady," Harol said.

When Jayne frowned in confusion, Richard explained, "We've been assigned as your personal guards until after Lord Ronen returns."

It was her turn to harden. Not saying another word, her pace quickened. *That whoreson! He's going to need to assign more than two men if he expects to keep me prisoner*.

11

"LADY JAYNE, it's been nearly two weeks." Queen Patricia frowned, staring at the noblewoman who'd been bound and gagged and now lay protesting on her bed. "Do you not think the time for these mischiefs has come to an end?"

Jayne glared at her and growled, "Mrumpinumph."

The queen sighed, sitting delicately on a chair to rub her temples. "I didn't think so."

"Murmamer." Jayne struggled to be free, but the knots binding her only tightened. It was probably a good thing no one could understand what she was saying. The sensitively feminine queen would undoubtedly have her drawn and quartered for her language. "Mumonmofamaf."

Jayne snorted. *Yeah, like I'm going to wax bloody poetic just to sound like some sort of flowery lady. I should have punched her when I had the chance. Damn you, Ronen, for leaving me here. Couldn't you have picked a nice, damp, dark prison cell? Surely being tortured on some sort of rack is better than this agony.*

"Fine." The queen dropped her hands into her lap as if coming to a decision. "I will just have to give you your lessons like this. Perhaps with a gag in your mouth you'll be able to actually listen to what I tell you and not aggravate me."

Oh, bloody misery, no! Jayne struggled harder, kicking and bucking on the bed. *Anything but this! Help! Ronen, remember the Caniba who held me prisoner? This is worse.*

"Let us speak about hair," the queen said, reaching to the table to pick up a comb. Jayne thought about crying. "A lady must never leave her chambers without first combing and styling her hair, preferably with the help of a servant. This also goes for when a lady finds herself staying in the encampments in her husband's tent near the battlefront. It gives the warriors a sense of pride and duty to have a visual of what they are fighting for. It is also a great honor to your family name to take pride in your appearance and manners." Putting the comb on her lap, the queen lifted her hands to pull at the fine clips holding her locks into place. "Should you find yourself without a servant, or mirror, it is up to you to still look your best." Long hair spilled over her shoulders. "I will now demonstrate a few simple techniques you can practice later. After today, I do not want to see your hair about your shoulders."

Jayne's eyes widened in horror and she tried to roll over so she didn't have to watch. This was worse than jumping into a portal right after a tough fight. In fact, she'd rather have the sensation of her bloody body being torn apart than sit through a full day of hairstyling lessons.

"If you look away, I'll only repeat myself," the queen warned. "I have no place to be. The king has ridden out to hunt with the men. The larders needed filling for winter."

Jayne growled but settled onto the bed, lying the best she could in her bound state.

"As with all rules there are exceptions," the queen continued, as if Jayne hadn't interrupted her. "In this case, if a lady finds herself under attack at night, whether it be in castle or encampment, there is clearly no time to attend personal matters. That would be selfish and vain and set a poor example for the women who will come after us. Only then is it acceptable to be seen undone. Oh, which brings me to the point of traveling by horseback overnight."

Oh, please, someone, anyone, kill me now.

"ALL CLEAR, MY LORD," Stephans said, reining his horse near Ronen's. "No fresh tracks along the west section and the ground is undisturbed. None of the Caniba people have risen from the earth."

Ronen nodded. With Stephans' arrival, all of the men had now reported in. The borderlands of Daggerpoint were secured. The Caniba queen concentrated her efforts further west at Spearhead.

"Double the patrol anyway," Ronen ordered, rubbing the back of his neck. He'd ridden hard, searching the forest in hopes of a battle—not that he wanted the Caniba to attack so close to the queen's and his wife's current residence. He just longed for an outlet to his pent-up frustrations. "I will not trust Sorceress Magda to leave these borders alone. She could be trying to focus our efforts at Spearhead only to attack here when our guard is down. It is possible she wanted us to find her spies in the forest."

"Yea, my lord," Stephans agreed. "I'll see to it."

As the knight rode off, leaving him alone, Ronen sighed. His body ached, not so much from being on his horse, but from the long, empty hours he spent pining for Jayne. How could he have been such a fool to tell her he cared for her when it was clear she wanted nothing from him? Each night that scene played in his head. What didn't play was a repeat of their connection. He waited for those moments when he would feel what she felt or see what she saw. Whatever the connection had been, it was gone now. As much as he longed to see her, he wasn't ready to go back.

"Those who are not staying, we ride for Daggerpoint Castle," Ronen ordered the small group. *I cannot avoid my lady wife forever.*

"ANY WORD?" Jayne rubbed her sore wrists absently as she slid in the seat next to Dersly. She peered over her shoulder to make sure they were alone. Her two guards sat three tables away as she commanded them to do whenever she was in the hall. If she had to be escorted by them all day and locked in her chambers at night, then she didn't want to have to eat with them too.

Dersly looked up at her upswept hair and pressed his lips tightly together to hold back his amusement. "Lessons going well, my lady?"

Jayne grunted.

"You are a vision of womanly—"

"Don't make me punch you again," Jayne grumbled, stealing Dersly's goblet to take a drink. She'd already confessed to him how miserable the queen's lessons on ladyhood made her. Dersly, being of a fighting mentality himself, well understood her pain. "Tell me, any news?"

She didn't have to explain what she inquired about. It was the same question she asked him every time she saw him.

"No word from Lord Ronen or his men," Dersly answered just as softly, lifting his hand to a servant to motion for another goblet. "Your husband is a great knight and leader. You should not let the men see you worrying about him."

"Do not give me the honor and duty lecture," Jayne warned. She scratched at her head, hating the way the weight was distributed toward her brow. It made her feel like she was about to fall face first onto the table. "I have had enough lessons and lectures to last a lifetime. I have half a mind to shave all the hair from my head after today. Let's see the queen try to test me on hairstyles tomorrow when I am bald."

Dersly frowned. "No, my lady, do not. I am sure Ronen would not—"

"I was jesting," Jayne drawled. "Besides, I tried it once. Easy to manage, but not pretty."

"My lady is always beautiful," Gerald announced, appearing across from her. He grinned and winked, taking a seat.

"Thank you, good sir," Jayne laughed, not taking anything the man said seriously. Gerald was a charmer, delightful and funny, but a charmer none-theless.

"What were we discussing?" Gerald asked, glancing expectantly between Dersly and Lady Jayne.

"My lady wished to challenge me to another drinking game," Dersly said.

Jayne laughed, appreciating his discretion. As far as she knew, he'd not told a soul about her inquiries into Ronen's health. For that she was grateful. After what Ronen said to her, she couldn't help but worry endlessly about him. People who cared for her never lasted long. "That is not true. I have had enough of this mead to last a lifetime. Besides, I have already proven myself capable."

"Is this when we tell her Lord Ronen ordered her cups watered down, and she does not hold her liquor as well as she thinks?" Gerald smiled innocently at Dersly.

"What?" Jayne gasped, looking to Dersly for confirmation. "He did not!"

Dersly merely took the goblet offered by a servant and chuckled into it as he drank.

"Oh! I can't believe that miserable lout did that!" she exclaimed, a little peeved at having her victory taken away.

"I can only assume you're talking about me."

Jayne tensed, her heart suddenly quickening. As many times as she imagined his voice, she didn't expect to hear it now. "Ronen?"

"My lord," Gerald greeted.

"Lord," Dersly repeated, nodding his head slightly.

Jayne turned to see Ronen standing behind her. Tired half-circles marred the flesh beneath his eyes, darkening them. Exhaustion radiated off him like heat. Almost stunned, she said to Dersly, "I thought you said there was no news."

"Methought there wasn't." Dersly shrugged. Then to Ronen, added, "Is all well at the borderlands?"

"Yea. Nothing to be alarmed about," Ronen answered, not taking his eyes from Jayne's face. The exhausted depths bore into her, but she wasn't sure what they were trying to express. Anger? Rage? Exhaustion? Nothingness?

Jayne grew uncomfortable under his scrutiny and automatically became defensive. "Are you worried that I'm without my guards? Don't. They're over there taking a break." She motioned behind him.

"Guards?" Ronen frowned. He started to speak, then shook his head as if it wasn't worth the effort to continue.

"My lord?" Jayne asked, wondering what was wrong with him. Maybe he was injured in a way she couldn't see. Well aware of how people stared, she refrained from asking. The truth was, she didn't know how to act. She'd put on a tough front for so long, she didn't know how else to be. Jumping up and hugging him was too out of character, even if every part of her being wanted to do just that. Then there was the fear—fear of what would happen to him if she allowed herself to get close.

"I go to rest." With that, he left her, walking around the table toward their chambers.

"I go to greet the riders. Since ordered to stay at the castle, I am starved for entertainment," Gerald said, pushing up from the table. He bowed, wishing them a good day before leaving.

"You are more like the people here than you know, my lady," Dersly commented when they were alone. "You have our hardness."

"What do you mean?" She looked at him in shock.

"You ask me fifty times a day about Lord Ronen's health, and when he appears, you show nothing of your emotions when I know you care for him deeply."

Jayne stared at her drink, as she contemplated denying it.

"What you do not have is our Starian sense," Dersly continued. "Life is to be lived, for it is a short time on this earth for a warrior. Go after your lord husband and give him some peace in this world. He should not have to wonder about your heart when he has the responsibilities of this country resting on him. If you truly care for him, you will be his constant. A man needs that, even if he doesn't say it."

"I thought I told you no lectures," Jayne mumbled, hating the wisdom in his words. "What makes you think you know anything about it? I see no constant in your life, unless Gerald—"

"My wife, stubborn wench that she was, never

told me until it was too late. Had I known she cared before her deathbed, I would have done things much differently. But I was young and foolish and still believed the honored teachings of the war gods I'd grown up hearing. It never occurred to me to confess an emotion I could not name. Warriors were not supposed to love, not romantically, not wholly. Now, methinks our people would do well to look at the other deities of our ancestors for guidance. It is why I find hope in you otherworlders. Perhaps you can reawaken our spirits and give us more to live for than war and death. Staria needs more love in its veins to go with the fire in its heart." Dersly stared at her until she was forced to meet his eyes. "Do not make the same mistake I made in my marriage, and do not wait for him to confess what he feels for you first. Most likely, he won't. He won't know how. None of us really do."

Jayne started to deny her feelings when the knight stood, cutting her off.

"I do not ask you to do anything that is not in you, but it would be good for this land if you could make your marriage work. Rumor has it Lord Ronen asked the king to stop all otherworld marriages through Divinity. I suspect it has something to do with you, otherwise he would not have urged a decision to be remade. There are several versions of the story, but the disheartened result is the same. Without Divinity, we'll have to go back to praying for women to fall through the fairy rings as gifts from the gods. Many men will die childless and without knowing the pleasure of a wife." Dersly cleared his throat, all sentiment falling behind the warrior mask. "Methinks I will find Gerald and see what news from the borders. Good day, Lady Jayne."

Dersly walked in the opposite direction Gerald had left from. Jayne watched him in silence until a servant appeared to clear the man's goblet. "Margaret, have food sent to Lord Ronen's chamber. He looked half starved."

"That would be the hard beef and bread they live on while riding. Horrible stuff, but it does its duty." Margaret nodded knowingly. "And for you as well?"

"No, thank you, just Lord Ronen." When she was again alone, Jayne's eyes trailed toward her bedchamber. She respected Dersly as a fellow fighter and they'd become friends over the last couple of weeks. But his words didn't change the fear she carried. He couldn't expect her to try to give hope to a country of knights. She barely got by for herself.

Run, Jayne, her thoughts whispered.

She didn't move. What if she ignored instinct

and stayed? What if she gave Ronen a try—a real try? If she were honest with herself, she did miss him while he was gone and had begun to miss the boxing ring even less. How did one compare what she did, fighting for money, to what these men did? They fought for honor and right. They didn't get paid an obscene amount of gold or get splashed across magazine covers. Their fame was earned by valor, not a well-paid camera man and creative biographer who invented a fake family for their little orphan street urchin.

Stay, Jayne, she consciously chanted. *Stay.*

Determined, and a little nervous, she finished her stout drink and stood from the table. Barely aware of her two guards right behind her, she forced her shaking legs to carry her across the main hall, through the passageway that seemed suddenly very long, and to the bedchamber door. Glancing behind her, she said, "Ronen is home now, you can stop following me."

"Not until the queen gives her order," Harol answered. "She was very specific, especially since you kept getting caught trying to leave the castle."

I was trying to hide from her lessons.

"The queen ordered me followed? Not Lord

Ronen?" Jayne asked. Harol nodded. "Why didn't you say?"

"My lady did not ask." Richard shrugged.

Jayne arched a brow, but refrained from arguing with him again. To do so would only be a way to run from what she needed to do. Pointing down the hall, she ordered, "Stay twenty paces away."

The men nodded, backing out of eavesdropping distance, but close enough to see her door should she try to come through it. Satisfied they wouldn't be listening, she slipped inside. Her eyes went hungrily to the bath, instantly finding Ronen amidst the curling steam.

"You were gone a long time," Jayne said, trying to figure out what exactly she wanted to say to him. *You were gone too long, Ronen. I missed having you in my bed. I thought about you. I fantasized about you. I'm glad you are safe. I worried about you. I sound like an idiot.*

"Not so long," he answered, not looking at her. Didn't he care she was there? She couldn't force her eyes off him as they devoured every visible inch. Her fingers flexed, itching to feel his flesh. Moisture pooled between her thighs, her sex aching to the point she adjusted her weight from one foot to the other in hopes of relieving some of the pressure.

"Did you," she paused, trying to think of anything that might get him talking, "fight?"

"No." Again, flat and emotionless.

"So, no Caniba?"

"No."

Jayne glanced over her shoulder at the door. It wasn't too late. She could run. Maybe this time Richard and Harol would be off their guard. Whatever sentiment Ronen had professed as he left her bed seemed to have dissipated like the steam rising above him. Hot one second, gone the next. "So, nothing happened?"

"I am exhausted, Jayne. What is it you wish to ask?" He still didn't look at her. She thought of taking her fingers through his damp hair and jerking his head back to force him to.

"I'm just making small talk." Then, cringing, she added, "The queen says that it's a lady's duty to inquire after her husband, I mean her man's, um, wartime activities."

Ronen gave a derisive laugh. "Since when do you care about being a lady?"

"I don't," she answered honestly before she could catch herself. "I mean, I've been taking lessons. Did you see my hair? I did it with only my fingers and touch of water."

"It's lovely." The words hardly sounded like a compliment.

"Yeah, I know I need some work. I keep feeling like my face is being pulled toward the ground." Jayne tugged at the locks, roughly pulling them down. He didn't seem to care either way, and there was no reason for her to be uncomfortable if he wasn't going to notice her efforts.

"Then take it down." Calm, logical and still not looking at her. One of her clips fell on the ground and she wanted to throw it at his head. Maybe violence would get his attention. She picked it up, bouncing it in her palm.

"Dersly promised to show me how to wield a sword if you said it was all right." Jayne sat on the bed, keeping her eyes on him. "He says it's well and good that a lady can throw a punch, but to truly be effective against an attack, she should be able to wield a blade."

"There is no reason. I will protect you," Ronen said. Finally, he moved to look at her and she felt a hopeful leap inside her chest. She held her breath. He arched a brow, drawling, "Unless it is me you wish to attack?"

"Why would I try to kill you?"

He turned his back on her once more, sitting as if

he hadn't moved. "To escape me because that is the only way I will let you out of our arrangement."

Jayne began to smile.

He continued, "The gods willed it for whatever reason and now it is our misfortune to bear."

Her smile dropped into a grimace. This conversation wasn't anything close to what she'd hoped. Sure, she didn't have clear plan for what she aspired to have happen between them, but if she did, this definitely wasn't it.

"That's a little harsh," she mumbled. "Clearly someone had a few weeks to brood."

"What?"

She didn't repeat the comment. Making a none-too-graceful transition, she rushed, "For the longest time I wasn't allowed to talk about my past because of the contract I signed with Divinity Entertainment. It had to do with the Public Appearance clause. Since my past was a bloody misery, I really didn't care if it stayed buried."

"What are you talking about?"

"The P.A. Department at Divinity. They wouldn't let me talk about my past until it became second nature not to say anything about who I was. But I suppose now if they kidnapped me and shipped me here, I'm probably no longer in contract. There are things in my life that I—"

He held up the back of his hand, cutting her off. "Jayne, if this is an attempt to leave me, please stop talking. As unfortunate as it is, I did not kidnap you and bring you here. You chose me at the ceremony. After witnessing the pain of my brother's first marriage, I had no plans to marry, ever, but you chose me and I accepted. Please, I'm exhausted and do not have the energy to fight with you tonight."

"No, I wanted to explain something, not fight. Would you just shut your mouth and listen? When I was little..." she paused in agitation. She hadn't intended to yell at him. Words jumbled in her head. Why did he have to interrupt her? She wasn't any good at this stuff. Calming her tone, she continued, "There was this girl, Clariah, and we entered the orphanage around the same time. After the first year, we both came to realize that we would never be adopted, which was for the best since the boys normally got taken to a workhouse and the girls became..." she grimaced, "used goods."

Ronen moved slowly along the edge of the tub, stopping when he was seated facing her. He looked at her, but said nothing. With those steady eyes on her, she now wished he'd turn around once more so she could talk to his back. Jayne found it ironic she wanted his full attention one minute only to dread it the next.

"Clariah was smart. Really smart." She pushed up from the bed and began to pace, moving her hands nervously before her as she spoke. "She could keep these complicated facts stored in her brain. She knew the exact time a guard would make their rounds on what day without even looking at a time-piece. She'd look at a new girl for two seconds and deduce what kind of person she'd be. She knew how the weather would affect Madam Gary's mood down to the degree. She calculated the number of days each month we'd go without food dependent on how many times Madam Timms smiled." Jayne stopped her story, explaining, "Madam Timms had a lot of male friends and when she met someone new, she always took the food money to buy a new dress and get her hair done."

"So you went without," he stated.

Jayne nodded. "We were rationed anyway and the food was terrible, so it wasn't so bad not to eat it."

His look said he didn't believe her. "You speak Clariah's name as if she is no longer. I take it you lost her?"

"It turned out she wasn't smart enough. After

we'd been there for three years, she planned an escape. It was supposed to be the two of us, but after seeing a new girl get beaten, we decided we had to take her with us. However, in our empathy, we misjudged her. Susan changed her mind and told Madam Gary in return for favors. That daughter of a whoring dog ended up becoming the child guard six months later. She'd sell out her own dead mother for an extra bit of bread and grog."

"Did you make it far when you escaped?"

"Oh, they let us crawl through air ducts, choke and burn ourselves in the smoke room, before scaling a snow-covered wall. Just as our bare feet touched free ground, they caught us. They could have stopped us before we started, but they wanted to teach us a lesson." Jayne gripped her hands tight. "Punishment for runaway orphans on my dimension was harsh. From the first day we arrived, we were told we were property of the central government, which was afraid we'd ruin their clean city streets. So instead we were swept away into these giant cement homes and kept out of society's eyepiece."

"What did they do to you?" His hand balled into a fist along the back of the bath, but he showed no other emotion.

"They beat us until the snow turned red, and

then they dragged us by our hair into a cell. They left us there for what had to be days. Clariah died the second night. One of the Madams had kicked her in the head. By the time the doctor arrived, an infection had set into my insides, and they had to scoop them out or I'd die as well. I often wondered why they bothered to save me. I would much rather have died. Clariah was like a sister. Without her, the place truly was hell."

"I'm sorry you lost her." His eyes softened, but she thankfully didn't see pity on his face.

"Thank you for not looking at me with sympathy. I don't tell you this to make you feel sorry for me."

"You only wished to explain how you cannot give me children," he concluded. "The robots cannot fix it?"

"The children thing is part of it," she admitted, "and no, the nanobots cannot fix what was not there when they were implanted. All they did was take away the surgery scars on my flesh. The biogeneticists confirmed it."

"And the other part?"

"I'm trying to explain it to you." She rushed on before he could interrupt. "After Clariah's death, I tried to escape every chance I got. I think I wanted to either be free or die trying. It's how I learned how to fight and take a punch. When finally I made it, I found the city streets weren't as clean as we'd been led to believe. An old woman found me and took me in. Having been an escaped orphan herself, Lotta understood there was little I could do to integrate myself into mainstream society. Everyone in my world is documented and scanned. For me to even try to get a job would mean I'd be captured and dragged back."

Jayne took a deep breath. Did he have to look at her like that? So intense and unmoving?

"Lotta came to care for me as a daughter and for a short time we were happy. But soon after I met her, she died from the cold. I took over her home until a couple of ruffians kicked me out. It really was just a small inlet in a delivery alley. I was alone and kept mostly to myself though I did find a nice little spot near the animal collective for a few months. The older orphans had taught the younger ones to read, so I spent my time memorizing the plaques. This kind guy found me reciting the information without looking and took me in. I don't know that I ever knew his real name, but I called him Mr. Bear. He was arrested that very week and I never saw him again— though I did walk by his place from time to time to see if he came back." She waved her hand at Ronen, shooing his eyesight away. "Can you not stare at me? It's hard enough thinking of these things without your eyes... Can you just not?"

His brow arched and he reached to dip his hand into some soap. Watching him lather suds over his tight flesh did little to improve her concentration. She pressed her legs tightly together, trying to end the throbbing ache of desire building there.

"Then there was Coach Wagner, the boxing trainer who discovered me..." Her gaze focused on his hands, gliding over strong, hard muscles. They moved over his arms and shoulders, across the expanse of his chest, up the hard cords of his neck. She swallowed, panting softly for breath. "...found me on the..."

Oh, bloody misery. She bit her lip. Ronen circled a hard nipple with the tip of his finger. She opened her mouth, wanting to bite his flesh. Jayne stepped toward the bath, her eyes sweeping down to look into the blue tinted water.

"Found you?" Ronen prompted, smiling slightly but still not looking directly at her, as she'd requested.

"I fought, I mean I learned to fight for pocket change and table scraps. They let me live in the boxer dorms. I kept my mouth shut and they put me on..." Jayne swallowed, wondering if he was at all hard beneath the surface. She wanted to take his cock deep as she rode his lap. "Divinity's entertainment circuit. Coach Wagner saw I could take a hit and took me under his training. Then..."

"Then?"

Jayne stiffened, frowning as she tried to get a hold of herself. She'd come to talk to him with a purpose and his sensual bathing movements were distracting her from it. Quite aware that her story was taking a long time to tell, she again tried to rush through. "He died, too. His heart gave out when he was out running the Animal Pass. Coaches aren't considered worthy of the expense of a full-body bioengineered upgrade, and he didn't have any nanobots inside him to repair the damage. Because of him I've earned a great living, more than anyone thought an orphan could amount to. I have money and fame and a place to live that I don't have to share. I even had that damned orphanage torn to the ground and Susan turned out into the streets. It was easier to do than I thought. I simply paid off dirty politicians to change the laws for better child treatment. They loved having something to campaign about."

"I do not think I would like your dimension," he

stated, his hands stalling on his chest. "I'm sorry you have suffered, but—"

"Wagner said he thought of me as family the night before he passed." She inched closer.

"But, here, there is no reason for you to suffer," he continued as if she hadn't interrupted. "You will be taken care of and, should I die, there are plenty of men who would seek you as a bride to ensure you are never without home or food. If you haven't noticed, women are prized treasures."

"Haven't you heard a thing I've said?" She came to the edge of the bath and couldn't help peeking down. His cock towered beneath the surface, erect and ready. "I can't stay here, Ronen. I'm not good for you or this country. I fight for money."

"Then try to run if you must, Fighting Lady Jayne." He surged forward, his hands striking out to grab her by her hips. He jerked her body forward, so his cheek pressed against her corset. "But I will follow you wherever you go. You will not escape me. Honor forbids it."

12

RONEN DID NOT KNOW what she meant to explain by telling her story. Why would anyone want to run back to a life that had caused her so much obvious loss and pain? Did she like to suffer? The look on her face when she spoke of her past belied the fact. Or did she seek comfort in the familiar?

His wet fingers dried against her thick skirts. Queen Patricia must have ordered his wife clothes, because her skirts had never felt so full. He didn't like it. The material kept his hands from molding along her thighs and ass. "I will confess that it amazes me how you claim to fight with your fists and yet your flesh is so beautifully unmarred. Methinks I would not like to see my battle scars healed. The length of a warrior's life is written on his body and scars are to be worn with honor." He reached over the bath, pulling at her skirts to lift them. Touching the back of her knee, he moaned. "But I find your smooth flesh very fitting for a lady, even one who can stand up to knights without fear."

Jayne leaned into him. Her hands grazed over his shoulders in light acceptance of his touch.

"Come." Ronen held her tight and pushed to his feet, lifting her up. "Let me see more of it. It has been too many days since I've felt your flesh around me, and my mood has soured because of it."

Jayne gave a surprised laugh and bent her knees so he could pull her over the edge. Then, letting her slide down his body, he lowered her into the water. Her gown pooled around her calves, engulfing his legs in the heavy material.

Pressing against him, she ran her hand through his hair and gazed into his eyes. "I'm glad you're unharmed."

It didn't appear that she tried to insult him, but the words cut. If she worried about him riding out to scout the borderlands, a rather unexciting task, what would she think of him riding off into battle? He'd led men into more than he could count, clearly always making it home alive, albeit sometimes with serious injuries. Then, as a thought occurred to him, he couldn't help giving her a lopsided grin. Did her concern mean she cared for him just a little? It was a small sign, to be sure, but he'd take it and gladly.

"Do not say such things in front of the men lest they think you worry. It would not do for them to believe that I am too soft to lead into battle." He found laces along her back and began following them with his fingertips to discover where they tied together.

"Soft?" She reached between them and grabbed his erection. "I don't think any part of you could be mistaken for soft."

Ronen groaned. He kissed her, feeling like a man possessed. There was comfort in avoiding the emotional and focusing on the physical. Every part of him needed more—more of her taste, her touch, her breath against his mouth. She'd gotten into his soul, entangling herself without even trying. He needed her like air and food, sure he would die without her. Words tried to form, but he didn't know how to say what he felt or if he even should. She made her position in his life clear.

I can't let you go, Jayne. I know I should let you choose your own fate, but I can't even consider it.

"I thought you were exhausted." Jayne walked him back and pushed him down into the water, completely unaware of the turmoil of thoughts warring inside him. His hands slid from her back, unable to find an opening to the corset.

I want to pull you into my chest and never let go. I want to lock you in a tower so I'll always know where you are. I want to see you smile. I want your happiness.

"How can a man sleep with you in his arms?" Ronen bit back the emotions, swallowing them deep and focusing on something he knew they got right—sex. The fatigue of his hard ride and sleepless nights seeped into nothingness. Her nearness gave him energy, fueling his passions and driving his need. She lifted her skirt so the ends floated over his thighs, tickling his flesh.

His heart beat a little faster as she took his face in her hands, angling his mouth for a kiss. Smooth legs brushed against him, sliding easily along his skin beneath the water. Jayne ran her hands wherever she could reach, exploring and massaging each muscle she came into contact with. He liked the feel of her soft skin, even though it covered a very athletic body.

Ronen closed his eyes and groaned as she rubbed his neck. Her kiss intensified, demanding he part his lips to allow her full access. He obeyed the silent command of her pressing mouth and probing tongue.

His hard erection tangled in her skirts and he reached to free himself.

Everything faded by the woman straddling his lap. His thoughts focused on her lips, the pants of her breath, her wet thighs. Heat centered over him as she lifted up. Her mouth slipped from his with a heavy sigh. As she maneuvered her body over his, he took hold of her hips, waiting for the glorious second he could impale her on his shaft.

Jayne made a weak noise of pleasure as the head of his cock found entrance. Ronen needed no more invitation. A fortnight had been one fortnight too long. He pulled her down as he angled his hips up. Her weight pushed him back down onto his seat and he groaned loudly.

His gaze met hers, holding it steady. There was a new softness to their depths, something he was sure he hadn't seen before when she looked at him. What had happened while he was gone? The expression gave him a hope he dare not feel.

Jayne moved slowly, as if treasuring each moment. He knew he was. Holding her waist, he let her have control. Her fingers ran through his hair, pulling lightly so he was forced to look up at her fully. Golden firelight illuminated her face. Their open mouths panted in unison, almost touching with each down thrust.

Time stood still for them, cocooning them in a single moment when nothing else mattered or even entered into his mind. It was just Jayne, just him, together as one.

As the tension built, her movements became fast and shallow. Her head rolled back on her shoulders, breaking the eye contact in her rapture. He felt her pussy quivering over his cock, gripping him tight and releasing. She let loose a short, high-pitched cry as she jerked with release. Ronen couldn't resist answering her call and came soon after, jetting his seed deep inside her.

Her forehead lowered, pressing into his. She didn't move from his lap, keeping his cock imbedded deep inside her sex. Harsh breath mingled between them. Ronen held her, not wanting to let go.

"Ronen?" She breathed against his neck. "I don't like the idea of someone else trying to claim me if you died."

Ronen frowned, unsure whether or not he'd actually heard the quiet words or if his pleasure-numbed mind invented them to soothe the desperate need inside his chest. She didn't move, didn't indicate she had spoken at all so he said nothing.

After a long moment, she pushed off his lap and stood. Wobbling as she gained her footing, she moved for the edge of the tub. When she stepped out, water dripped from her gown, pooling loudly onto the stone floor.

"Then I must try not to die," he said, trying to make her smile while trying to find the words to make her stay. But tender words only seemed to make her uncomfortable and he wanted so much to please her. When she spoke, Ronen saw that it had taken a lot for her to tell him of her past. However, her words didn't tell him what he needed most to know—what she was thinking. Did she feel anything for him? Or did his tired mind just imagine it in her, grabbing onto any reason to hope? Or perhaps it was his needy heart that saw what it had to see? Then again, maybe she only thought of escape, of leaving him, of freedom from Staria.

How could he hold onto her when she didn't want to be with him? How could he force her to accept what she didn't want? And, most tragically, how could he even think of letting her go?

As if she hadn't heard his words over the swishing of her heavy skirt across the floor, she said, "I should find something dry to put on and fix my hair. Queen Patricia threatened to draw and quarter me, or chop off my hands, or some such nonsense if I ever showed up 'unladylike' in her hall again. Though, I wonder what she'd do if I paraded around naked. Perhaps it would give her a very delicate attack and she'd never bother me again."

She closed the door without a backward glance, leaving a trail of wet stone behind her. Ronen didn't move from the tub, too exhausted at the moment to even think of a reply.

$$\times$$

JAYNE TOOK A DEEP BREATH, pressing her back against the door. She hoped her parting words appeared light and carefree because inside she felt like she'd been stabbed a thousand times. She'd opened herself to him and he said nothing. Now that it was over, her hands shook violently and she balled them into fists.

Though, to be fair, her mind seemed to run in circles until she couldn't remember exactly what she said to Ronen. She told him her story, but did she make her point? Did she say what she needed to say? Did he understand why she needed to leave him?

It was no wonder the man was confused. She tried to explain that she was no good for him even as she tried seducing him. He'd been naked and so incredibly alluring in his bath. How could she resist going to him? How could she think?

People who cared for her never lasted long. Sure, some carried on for a few years, but she didn't want to wait around to learn he died in battle. Then, what? Another man would take hold of her and say, "mine"? She'd thought that at least here, in a war-hardened land filled with warriors, a man like Ronen would never come to have feelings for her. Or had those feelings gone away? She wasn't sure which answer was worse. Had she known she'd end up here, confused and tearful, she'd never have chosen her original plan of claiming him and seducing him. It was never supposed to go like this.

"I rambled," she whispered, trying to make sense of the rush of words she'd thrown at him before resorting to sex to avoid saying more. "I didn't say it right. I need to go back and make sure he understands."

Her wet gown stuck to her legs, but instead of changing, she went back into his chamber. She looked at the bath, but it was empty. Scanning the room, she found him stomach down on the bed, naked.

"I'm afraid if I stay here, you'll die," she blurted,

her voice soft. "Logically, I know it's stupid and that there is no such thing as a person being cursed, but I can't help it. I'm really confused. I don't want to lose more people and I think losing you might hurt unbearably. I hate you for making me feel anything. I was doing fine on my own. I had a life and security. But you see Dersly said I should come tell you, but I'm not convinced it's such a great idea. So..."

Jayne inched closer to the bed. He hadn't moved.

"Ronen?" Jayne leaned over, seeing his closed eyes lined with the purple of exhaustion. She gave a derisive laugh and backed toward her chamber and shut the door between them. "Oh, of course, you're asleep. I finally get the nerve to tell you I love you and you're sleeping. Maybe it's a sign that this isn't meant to be. Maybe here your gods really do have a plan and I ruined it by speaking up at the ceremony. I'm sure they have a nice, wholesome ladylike woman for you, Ronen, someone who can make you proud and be your constant. You deserve that much."

Jayne pulled at her corset laces, pushing the tight bodice over her hips to the floor. In irritation, she kicked at the stiff material so it flew into a wall with a splat. "For a place that's so sexual, they make it impossible to get out of their dresses."

Her hands fumbled on her gown and, with each

effort to undress, she became more incensed, focusing her anger on the clothing so she didn't have to feel anything else. She flung her limbs wildly, clawing and cursing to get out of her wet gown. It stuck to her legs, itching uncomfortably.

"This dimension has messed with my head. I have to get out of here. Once I leave, it'll all go back to the way it should be." She heard a rip and pulled harder. The back split open and her gown gaped along the bodice. Tugging and kicking, she finally managed to free herself. She gasped for breath, panting from her tirade. "When I find the son of a whoring Divinity cat who did this to me, I'm going to rip him apart. He's going to discover just how tough Fighting Lady Jayne can be. I don't need Ronen. I don't need anyone."

As if all the energy was suddenly drained out of her, she sank to the chilled stone floor. A tear slipped over her cheek and then another.

Please just let me go home. I don't want to feel, not this. I don't like being scared or out of control. Please, Divinity, just let me come home.

THE ACHE that settled inside of her chest didn't

fully go away. Jayne had given herself the chance to say how she felt, and she doubted she'd work up the nerve again. The more she thought about Ronen's attitude in the bath, the more she was able to convince herself that his two weeks away from her had purged whatever feelings he thought to have. That or she'd dreamt the words in the first place.

Thinking about it made the pain worsen until the unusual threat of tears burned her nose and moistened her eyes. Jayne didn't want to cry, or feel, or be in Staria. She wanted the cold, lonely, fighting existence she'd built for herself. Adored by many, known by none.

Quit lying to yourself, her heart scolded. *You know as well as I that we don't want to leave him.*

Stuff it, you bloody miserable, overactive, overemotional, treacherous organ, her brain screamed back. *Home is where we belong.*

He is where we belong. He is home. Damn her feeling heart.

He is not safe. We cannot take losing him. We cannot go through the pain of losing again. You know as well as I that everything we love dies in the end. Damn her logical brain.

For something that's supposed to think, you're a

very stupid brain. Everything eventually dies. It doesn't mean we can't live.

"Great, I've truly gone mad," Jayne mumbled.

"I should say. You're wearing down the stone floor like a woman possessed."

Jayne frowned, turning a rueful mask to the queen. The lady stood watching her pace the narrow side passage from the archway. She was immaculate in dress and regal in manners as always. Eager for an outlet and knowing a fight to be her easiest release, she said, "You better have your goons with you because I'm not coming to another lesson right now willingly."

Patricia chuckled softly, not giving her the argument Jayne was brewing for. "Seeing your hair and dress, I would say my lessons are doing you no good. But, hearing your argument with yourself, I would say you have much more on your mind than hair and dress. I forgot what it was like to be newlywed and unsure of your place."

"I don't know what you mean," Jayne lied. Had she been having her brain and heart argument out loud? How humiliating. Could this day get any worse?

"I'll send you back," the queen said.

"Excuse me?" Jayne stiffened in disbelief.

"To your dimension." Patricia tilted her head to the side, her eyes steady. "I have the power to send you back."

No.

"Why would you do that?" Jayne didn't dare move.

"To save you from the insanity that threatens. To protect the House of Firewall from another unhappy marriage. To replace you with a lady who wishes to be a lady and will not embarrass the proud tradition of Starian nobility." The queen walked slowly around Jayne, eyeing her. Jayne turned in a circle, returning the stare with an unpleasant one of her own. "Or perhaps it is because I simply do not want you here."

Jayne clenched her fists.

"Relax," the queen laughed, unaffected by the posturing. "The last reason was a jest. In truth, I find you amusing in your willfulness and the knights respect your strength. If you stayed, wholeheartedly stayed, methinks you could be a fine lady wife. But, if this dimension will take your sanity, then you should leave and spare Lord Ronen the agony of watching you deteriorate."

No. And you can't make me.

"What about your traditions? The ceremony?

The whole mentality of not rethinking a decision once it is made?" Jayne waited, silently begging the woman to force her to stay.

"The choice is yours, my lady," the queen said instead, walking out the way she'd come. "Stay or go back through the portal."

Jayne stared after her. Then, the slight tap of footfall sounded behind her, firm yet soft, drawing her attention. Ronen crossed his arms. He looked rested but for the turbulent storm churning in his gaze.

"The queen is wrong," Ronen stated. "I do not know what game she plays, but I suspect she thinks to jolt you into a decision. However, she does not have the power to end our marriage. Only death or the gods can do such a thing."

"Or you," Jayne said. "But you will never let me go."

"You chose me. No woman has ever stated her claim to a man." Ronen studied her, as if searching for something he couldn't find. "Perhaps there is a reason for that. So be it. You win."

When he turned to leave with those cryptic words, she rushed forward to stop him. "So be what?"

"You can go home. Perhaps the House of Fire-wall was not meant for happy marriages. Perhaps the gods have been speaking and I've just been too stubborn to listen." He refused to look at her, even as she tried pulling on his arm to make him. "Go home, Jayne. Go back to your life and forget this place ever existed."

Just like that he changes his mind? He is giving up?

"Ronen," Jayne stated, desperate to get his attention. He tried to step forward, but she blocked his path. Fear gripped her and she wanted to shake him until he took the words back. He was giving her what she'd wanted but Jayne hardly felt victorious. If he wouldn't look at her, she'd get in his face and make him. His hard gaze stared over her shoulder. "Are you... What I mean to say is—"

"Sorceress Magda's warriors press upon our borders. She's the strongest leader we've seen in tens of years. I do not have time to fight with a bride, Jayne." He glanced at her before quickly staring down the hall once more. His jaw tight, he continued, "I do not have time to chase you all over the countryside. If I were but some foot soldier, such a luxury might be mine, but I'm a leader. Men look to me as an example, and it is better for my family name to have you gone than to have you constantly embarrassing me. It was a mistake to try and force you to stay. The whole trade agreement with Divinity was a mistake. Go home. It's what you want. When my men ride tonight, I ride with them and we will never see each other again."

"I thought the Starians didn't second-guess decisions." Why wouldn't he look at her?

Great going, you stupid brain! You over thought and now it is too late, her heart yelled.

Bloody fucking misery, her brain mumbled.

"We are not so foolish as to force a decision out of pride," he answered. "Besides, your presence proves Divinity cannot be trusted. I will not put others through a false marriage."

"What about you?"

"I'm a warrior. It's time I got back to being just that."

Jayne refused to move. Well, refused was a lie. The truth was she couldn't move. The weight of her limbs became impossible to lift. Ronen's words stung. She'd begged endlessly for him to let her go home, to give her freedom. She'd fought for this moment, and now that she had everything she'd pleaded for, she wanted to scream in agony at having received it.

"Ronen," she tried to speak. Her throat tightened and it became hard to breathe. Her brain seemed to spin in dizzying circles inside her head.

"The king orders that I ride at once," he said. "I will have Dersly escort you back to Battlewar Castle where the Divinity portal is kept. We were left with instruction as to how to contact them should the need arise. I'll send orders that you are not to be stopped. All I ask is you act with dignity before you go. Once through that portal, your life is your own and what happened here will be a distant memory."

"Ronen," she whispered, trying again to put into words what she felt. The problem was, she wasn't sure how to. "What will you tell people?"

"That's my concern."

"But—"

"Good journey, Lady Jayne." He lifted his hand as if he might touch her but then let it drop to his side. "And may you fight with honor."

He stepped around her and left. She stood, frozen, as his footfall echoed behind her before disappearing completely. Ronen set her free. No, he did more than that. He practically shoved her through the portal toward her freedom.

"Ronen, stop, I don't want to go," she whispered. But her throat was too tight and no sound came out. He'd just given up. Jayne knew she couldn't blame him. She'd fought him since that first day out of pride and stupidity. Part of her had never thought he'd give in.

Her mind raced, but she had no solution. The queen wouldn't stop her. Ronen wouldn't stop her. If royalty and her husband sent her back, no one would think to stand in her way.

Husband.

Jayne shivered. She'd never allowed herself to think of Ronen as a husband. Sure, others said it, but never her. She felt the walls inside her begin to crumble, but it was too late.

"Oh, bloody misery, Ronen." Jayne sank to her knees, trembling violently as tears rolled over her cheeks. How could she have been so blind? "I have truly made a mess of my life this time."

13

Ronen had faced terrible odds in battle. He'd seen death and made hard decisions. He'd been wounded and had nearly died on numerous occasions. Yet, none of those life experiences had come close to using the reserve of strength it took to say good journey to Jayne.

When he heard the queen's offer to set her free, he'd thought to deny it and never let her go. That is what his instinct told him to do. Queen Patricia had no authority to end his marriage, and Ronen had no clue as to why she said as much. Such things were the matters of gods, above men and royalty. But then he looked into Jayne's face, so full of emotions he'd never seen there before, ones he couldn't read. In that moment, he knew he'd lost the most important battle of his life. Somehow, he'd always known she'd win, that he'd give in to her and let her go, even if the act ripped out his heart.

I am a leader of men. A warrior. A knight. The battlefield is my life. War is my mistress. I am not meant for softer things.

His heart was one wound that would never stop aching, but hopefully with enough time it would harden and scar. Already he felt a fine rage settling inside his chest, urging him to strike out, to fight, to scream, to ride into Sorceress Magda's encampment and die a hero.

Unfortunately, the location of Magda's encampment was unknown, and any battles to be fought were days away from where he now rode through the forest with the small contingency of knights. The only enemy his sword could face was the bark of a tree, and his men might look at him strange were he to jump off his mount and attack yet a fourth hapless trunk.

"This clearing is as good as any other, my lord. A stream is nearby." Sir Thomas said, venturing next to him. "Should we make camp?"

"Further," Ronen grunted. Thomas slowed and backed away, not arguing. Ronen nudged his horse, urging it to run. If he couldn't fight his demons with a sword, he would try to run them ragged.

$$\times$$

"IT PROVES you can never predict the actions of a Starian warrior." Queen Patricia placed her hand on Jayne's shoulder. "Methought my decree would have a different effect on you two, but I see you are just as stubborn as he."

Jayne eyed the woman. Part of her wanted to hate Patricia for prompting the end of her marriage. Whatever the queen intended with her offer to send Jayne home clearly had not worked.

"Dersly is waiting," Jayne mumbled, purposefully turning her attention to where the big knight stood by two horses. His blank expression stared back at her, but she didn't need to see his emotions to know he was disappointed with her. "Thank you for your hospitality."

The queen arched a brow, but Jayne didn't correct her statement. Ronen's last request had been for Jayne to act with dignity and she intended to do just that.

"Your hair looks very nice swept off your shoulders. It's the first time I've seen you looking the part of a true Starian noblewoman. I'm proud to see my lessons were not all ignored. Safe travels, Fighting Lady Jayne." The queen backed away several steps before turning to go inside the castle.

Jayne strode over the hard dirt path through the courtyard, trying not to break down again. She'd cried when Ronen left her in the hallway and as she'd watched him ride out of the main gate the night before. She'd wept through most of the night, curled on the hard floor and only falling asleep from pure emotional exhaustion. Never had she felt so miserable. Never had she felt so helpless and alone.

How was she going to live the rest of her life without him?

"I'm a fool," she whispered to herself.

Dersly grunted. "I will not disagree, my lady." He handed her the reins to her horse and cupped his hand to help her up. Jayne eyed the animal wearily. "It's a sweet mare. She'll not throw you and I'll ride slowly."

Jayne placed her foot on Dersly's cupped hands and considered asking for a wild, untamed mare that would trample her the second she tried to climb on its back. "Thank you, Dersly."

✕

"Do you hear singing?" Jayne frowned, tilting her head to the side as the faint hint of voices roused her from her depressed thoughts. She hadn't said a word as they rode from Daggerpoint Castle, through the quiet encampment of solemnly and somewhat accusatory gazes of the knights. The forest even seemed dead to her, even though the soft hum of insects and the infrequent call of a distant bird interrupted the solitude.

Dersly glanced at her and she half expected him to be surprised that she spoke. Instead, his steady gaze met hers and he nodded once. "It is most likely travelers engaged in a little merriment on their way through the forest, but I will have to check it out. You should stay back."

Jayne laughed dryly. "Last time I was alone in this forest, I was chased by crazed boars and captured by man-eaters. Not that I can't take care of myself, mind you, but I think I'll come with you all the same."

Dersly grunted, nudging his horse to move faster. Her mare automatically kept pace without having to be directed. It was a good thing. Though she could keep her ass planted firmly in the saddle and hold on, she really didn't know much of the nuances of riding.

If the beast were to take off at a dead run, she'd most likely take her chances jumping off the side.

The singing became louder and evidently more drunken in tone. Mismatched pitches rose and fell, some of the voices pausing at odd moments as if to take another drink. The lyrics, barely recognizable, were about some magical lady riding into battle and ending the war with her magical...

Jayne strained, trying to hear, but the uncontrolled laughter muddled the ending. If it made these burly sounding men so giddy, it had to be something dirty. Just as she was about to ask about it, one voice rose high above the others.

Ronen!

The instant rush of pleasure she felt instantly became replaced by rage. Unsure what she was doing, but too mad to care, she nudged the horse's side as she'd seen others do and held on tight as it shot forward past a startled Dersly. He reined to the side, letting her by.

Jayne wasn't sure how she managed, but after a few heart-thumping seconds, she broke into a clearing. Rounded eyes turned toward her. A few of the men grabbed their swords and dropped their jugs, ready to do battle.

"Stop!" Jayne yelled at the horse. She jerked on

its reins and it slowed. Seeing she was riding past, she whipped her leg over the side and leapt off the animal's back. She hit the ground with a hard thud and the wind rushed from her lungs.

"What? Jayne?"

Inhaling deeply, she surged to her feet, running more on adrenaline than anything else. The skirt of the gown wrapped her legs, causing her to stumble as her foot caught on a leaf-covered branch. Jayne cursed it, righting herself as she scanned the clearing for Ronen.

"Battle?" She swept her arm over the stunned group of men. "You had to go fight in battle?"

"Jayne," he stammered as her eyes finally found him. He held up his hands defensively in front of him, as if to stop whatever it was she was going to do to him. Bloody misery, he looked great, handsomer than that moment she first saw him in the hall. How could he have thought to send her home? How could she have thought to leave him?

She ignored the sound of Dersly's voice and the drunken murmurings of the knights. Ronen didn't move, though his lips stayed parted as if he would speak. Dark waves framed his face, falling to his shoulders. His black tunic molded the thick muscles of his chest and waist, muscles she could picture as easily as if she looked at him naked. She knew the location of every scar, could bring to mind the exact feel of his heartbeat beneath her hand and the sound of his voice catching the second before he met with climax.

In the short time she'd been there, she knew this man better than she'd really known anyone. He'd broken through her guard, pierced her soul. Perhaps she'd always known he would, from that first moment she saw his eyes, dark and deep and expressive. She knew then that she'd have to be careful of those eyes.

Well, now he'd have to be careful of her!

"You miserable son of a..." Jayne didn't stop as she stormed across the small encampment. Desperately needing to kiss him, she instead balled her fist and punched. It snapped against his jaw hard, throwing his head back. "That's fighting." She kept after him, hitting him in the gut. "This is fighting!"

"Jayne!" he ordered, catching her fist in his hand before she could land a third blow.

She tore her hand away from his touch. "You miserable coward How dare you think you can just send me away and come hide in the forest?"

"I'm not hiding," he defended, his initial shock replaced by a frown.

"Please, you're drunk in the middle of the woods

having a sing-along with the all-boys choir over there." In disgust, she waved her hands over the group of knights. "And all the while, I'm in agony because I've been banished."

"Banish—"

"I can't believe you're out here in the woods." Her words lost some of the venom as she looked to the trees. The steady trunks and dancing limbs held no answers.

"What are you doing here, Jayne? Methought you wanted to go home. Methought I was giving you everything you'd asked for."

"I did want to go home. I do." She growled. Anger she could do, but it would seem she still wasn't great at this part. "But only to gather my belongings, and for the selfish reason of avenging my name by kicking Big Bobby and his father's asses. After that, I want to go home with you. I want to do the thing with the orphans and the rebuilding of Firewall Castle so I don't have to live with the queen. I want one bed, no more of this two rooms nonsense. On my side, I want a hard, stiff mattress and on your side you can have your fluffy softness. And I don't want to style my hair every morning and I want my own clothes. I've had enough of these corsets. I can't run in a skirt."

At the last bit, he smirked. "You can't dismount either. I saw your landing from the horse. And I like your hair."

"Well, tough," she blustered. "I like it down or pulled back, not up."

"Are we fighting about your hair now?" Ronen crossed his arms, but any menacing in the stance was taken away by the subtle shifting of light in his eyes. "What is it you want, Jayne? You ran from me, endlessly. You begged me to send you back to your dimension. You fought me at every turn."

"I fought out of pride because I never thought you'd let go, but I was wrong. You let go and I hate it." The more she spoke, the more she realized she did know what she wanted. "I want you, Ronen. Just you. Well, you and that other stuff, but mostly you, my lord husband. I want a life here."

Ronen took a hesitant step forward. Jayne heard snickering and glanced to where their audience watched, captivated and amused. Dersly was the only one grinning openly, as he nodded his head in approval.

"I want you, too, Jayne," he whispered, drawing her gaze back to him with a gentle hand to her cheek. "But I refuse to spend any part of our marriage with one of us chasing after the other. I need to know you're sure, that you won't change your mind. I can't have doubts in my head when I'm away at battle."

At his admission, a rush of pleasure flooded her, carrying with it the barely suppressed desire that always simmered near the surface. "I don't want you to have doubts about my loyalty to you. I want you to be safe and careful so that you'll always come home to me. Because, if you don't, I swear I'll kill myself and come after you into the next life before I let another man claim me."

The pleasure in his gaze warred with concern. "You will never harm yourself." The words left no room for argument.

"Then you had better always come home. You promised to protect me, my lord, and I'll hold you to it." Knowing if she kissed him, she'd not be able to stop, she gave him a meaningful smile and leaned closer, dropping her tone to whisper, "Are you sure there will be no chasing in our marriage, my lord?"

When she pulled back, he watched her intently, not answering. Jayne backed toward the trees, keeping her eyes on him as she led him away from the group. The second her meaning became clear, he sprang into action, darting after her.

"We'll leave you to it, Lord Ronen," one of the drunken knights called after them.

"Unless you need help capturing the Fighting Lady," another added, which caused a fit of drunken laughter and a stern scolding from Dersly about respect.

Jayne chuckled, not bothered by the men's good-natured teasing. She ran faster, absentmindedly dodging through the trees, leaping over logs and ducking low-hanging limbs. Realizing she didn't hear Ronen's pounding feet chasing after her, she began to slow, her smile slowly dying on her lips.

"Captured," Ronen exclaimed as he emerged from the trees to grab her by the arms and pull her tight to his chest. Her heart pounded, more from the excitement than from the run. He'd barely broken a sweat and his breath was steady, but she felt the beat of his heart hammering in time with hers.

Pleasure erupted every place their bodies touched. Jayne focused on him and only him. When she looked into his eyes, the rest of the world didn't matter—not Divinity or her boxing career, not Bossman or his oaf of a son, not the Starian war or her past. All that mattered was Ronen and the life they would have together. And Jayne planned on fighting to her very last breath to keep it.

"Captured," she repeated, nodding her head. "Always."

Ronen grinned, his captivating eyes keeping hers locked in their magical pull. The hard length of him pressed against her, leading to the unmistakably thick outline of his cock. He kissed her and she moaned, wrapping her arms around him. Ronen knelt, pulling her down with him so that their knees pressed into the damp earth below. Leaves rustled in the treetops, as the forest seemed to enclose them in its private hold.

Their lips joined in a soft, exploring embrace. Jayne sighed. "You taste like mead." When he would stop, she moaned in protest. "No, I like it."

His kiss instantly deepened as his lips devoured hers. Ronen pulled at her corset, loosening it so she could pull it over her head and toss it aside. Without the constricting material, she breathed deeper. He gripped the gown at the small of her back, tugging but unable to pull it all the way up with her knees trapping the skirt. Giving up with a grunt of frustration, he instead found hold on her clothed breasts, massaging them through the bodice of her gown. The strong fingers rubbed in firm strokes, budding her nipples into his palms.

Jayne swayed back and forth, pulling at her skirt until it was finally free from her knees. With his fumbling help, she managed to wiggle out of it.

Ronen snapped it in the air, laying it over the ground behind her. Now that she was naked, she set to work on the laces of his black tunic. It was the same warrior style she'd stolen from him the night they met and she had to admit, the outfit looked much better on him.

The hem of his shirt tickled her breasts as he lifted it over his head. Jayne eagerly explored his chest with her hands and mouth, trying to touch every muscle and trace every scar. She wanted to feel all of him at once, needed him to feel her. Ronen unfastened the laces at his waist, loosening his breeches. A twinge of anticipation worked over her, centering on her sex. Her pussy ached to be filled.

Jayne gripped his hair, forcing their mouths to join. She thrust her tongue into the warmth of his mouth, tasting the delicious flavor of his mead-laden tongue. She'd been so worried she'd never see him again as she rode from Daggerpoint, and now poured all that emotion into her touch. Panting against his mouth, she whispered, "I love you, Ronen."

He moaned into her, leaning so she was forced back onto the ground. The cool breeze was no match for the heat of his body. Her gown, padded by fallen leaves, crackled beneath her as she moved, creating the perfect bed.

Jayne hooked her legs around his waist, rubbing her thighs along his hips to push down his loosened pants. She loved the strong texture of his skin as muscles bulged in all the right places. He reached between them, cupping her sex with his warm palm. Ronen stroked the clit he found buried within the slick folds. Each stroke of a calloused finger made her jolt a little inside until she was moving restlessly against him in desperation.

"Methought I would never feel you again." He drew his lips along her jawline, nipping and licking a hot trail from her chin to her ear. Sucking on the lobe, he groaned and forced a finger up into her sex. Wiggling it inside her, he continued, "I was sure I'd die from wanting you."

"Then why did you send me away." Jayne gasped and arched, trying to hear his words but torn between the pleasure and need for concentration.

"To make you happy. My pain is nothing compared to your happiness." He moved his finger faster, adding a second to the first while his thumb pressed over her clit. She jerked, squirming frantically for release. Ronen had found that sweet spot and worked it mercilessly.

"Ronen, I..." She gasped, unable to say what she meant as a long incoherent mumbling sounded from her throat. *Ronen, I'm happiest when I'm with you.*

Jayne clawed at his back with one hand as she reached for his wrist with the other. She forced his fingers from inside her before grabbing his cock and guiding it to the mouth of her sex. With a pant, she thrust up, urging him inside her. He obeyed, thrusting to the hilt.

As if unable to hold back his own desires, Ronen rocked wildly on top of her. He braced his arms on either side of her, slamming his hips in a primal rhythm. Jayne took everything he gave and returned it. Sunlight framed his body from above, slightly shaded by the treetops. The sweet smells of nature, pure and perfect, infused with the masculine scent of his flesh.

"Jayne." Her name sounded rough and loud from his lips as his body tensed. She came a second later, trembling violently in release. Ronen's body strained as he jerked a few more times. Then, with a shortened yell of victory, he too found his end.

When the tremors subsided, he fell to her side and cradled her against him.

"I could do that forever." Jayne yawned, closing her eyes. The stress of their fight had ebbed from her body. That, combined with sexual pleasure, left her spent.

"I told you the gods knew what they were doing." Ronen held her close, not looking as if he planned on moving to rejoin the encampment anytime soon.

Jayne merely smiled, perfectly content. "Perhaps they did."

EPILOGUE

"I KNOW I said we could raise a houseful of orphans, but don't you think we should rebuild Firewall first so we have somewhere to put them?" Ronen eyed the three little boys his wife had collected on their journey through Staria. She'd insisted on rerouting the drunken party of knights, taking a trip to every village between Daggerpoint and Battlewar, even if that village was a half-day's ride out of the way. A journey that should have been a matter of days, took weeks.

"What?" Jayne demanded, turning to look at him from where she stood next to the controls to the Divinity portal. She appeared to know what she was doing as she pressed the buttons and turned the many dials.

Turning her attention to the three dark-headed brothers, she asked, "You all don't care that we don't have a castle yet, do you? Hughe? William? Tree?"

The three boys quickly shook their heads in denial. They didn't say much, especially the youngest, Tree, who wasn't much older than three. After the tragedy they'd witnessed while living in the isolation of the forest borderlands, Ronen couldn't blame them. After their parents were murdered in front of them, they'd been shipped from family to family. None of the borderland peasants had the resources to care for three young ones for very long periods of time, though they'd done their best.

"See, they're fine. I'm fine. Are you fine?" She arched a meaningful brow, and he knew she wanted him to reassure the children they were wanted.

Ronen cleared his throat, still not completely used to the affections his wife wanted him to express toward the children. "Yea. I'm pleased to have such fine boys."

They merely stared back at him in confusion that he'd say such an unmanly thing. Oh, the things a man would do to please a wife.

"Why don't you take them out to the fire ceremony we saw them building outside? Or help them get settled into the spare room in the Mace Tower while I handle this." She turned her attention back to what she'd been doing.

"I'm not leaving you alone," Ronen stated. Jayne smiled, but didn't argue.

The portal was kept hidden in a special room beyond the old iron-door prisons, very unlike the cell Jayne had been kept in upon her arrival. Ronen almost laughed at himself for believing Divinity's lies about keeping the women locked up while they adjusted to the new dimension.

The room was more of a cave, hand dug especially for the portal to keep it hidden beneath the castle in an underground clearing. At the end of the clearing, a large domed vault had been constructed by Divinity to reflect the architecture of the castle. A soft blue glow shone onto the portal from the far, high corner of the cave.

"How does it work?" William, the middle child asked his oldest brother softly.

"Magic," Hughe responded, confident in his answer.

"That's right," Jayne said. "Magic."

Ronen suppressed a laugh. For someone who fought really hard not to be part of a family, she took to mothering better than any woman he'd ever seen— especially to children who were not her own blood.

"That should do it," she announced, pressing one last button before backing away from the controls to stand beside Ronen. She wore a pair of breeches and a tunic shirt tailored for her smaller frame. Even a small knife graced her waist, at his insistence. Though she swore she didn't need it and that her fists would do just fine.

"How do you know it will work?" he asked.

She angled her body so she stood before the boys. "I used the secure code for Divinity's head of entertainment and offered to let him hold a warriors' battle challenge here in Staria with the promise of so much money he'd not be able to refuse coming himself to seal the offer."

Ronen covered his mouth and coughed loudly, warning the soldiers he'd ordered to hide in the stairwell to be on alert. Jayne might think she could take on all of Divinity with her fists, but he wasn't taking any chances with her life. After a few minutes, the light on the portal began to shift from blue to a light gold.

Ronen saw his wife grin. "We're just going to talk to them, right, Jayne?"

"He's coming." Jayne lifted her hands to her hips and stared at the center light. A dark shadow began to appear.

"Uh, Jayne, right?" Ronen persisted, wondering why he hadn't demanded she promise to behave when he had the chance.

Oh yea, she started kissing my stomach and I forgot.

He swallowed hard, refusing to listen to his suddenly very interested cock.

Jayne's grin widened as a smiling figure emerged. "Go hide in the stairwell, boys, and see how your new mom kicks a little otherworlder ass."

The End

KEEPING PAIGE

THE SERIES CONTINUES...

Divinity Warriors Book Three
by Michelle M. Pillow

Alternate Reality Romance

An outcast because of her psychic abilities, Paige doesn't expect her people to rescue her when a zealous sect of Faerians sacrifices her to their gods. Thrown through a fairy ring to a new dimensional plane, drugged on ambrosia, she is compelled to claim the first man she meets. Only when the effects wear off and she's left with a husband expecting more than she's willing to give, does Paige discover the true extent of what the fairies have done.

Ordered by the king to marry, Sir Aidan of Fallenrock is dead set against taking a bartered bride. He believes his people should be patient and wait for the gods to bless them. When the beautiful Lady Paige comes through the sacred rings, kissing and touching him like she knows their joined fate, Aidan's sure he's being rewarded—until his new bride tries to back out of their marriage.

Keeping Paige Prologue Excerpt

Great Forest, Faerian Territory, Parallel Universe

"Oh, blessed fairies of the great forest, givers of spring, and givers of life after the cold! Take our autumn offering to grant us safe winter and bring life after the snow. Take our offered sister and make her a queen of your realm."

"Let me go, you crazed heretics!" Paige screamed, kicking and jerking her limbs to be free of the hands that held her high over a sea of ivy-crowned heads. Outrage pumped hard and fast through her veins until she felt as if her heart might burst from her chest in little pieces. "You don't want me. I'm not a believer. I will curse you with dead trees and wilted flowers. My father's people will not stand for this!"

All right, so the last part was a lie. Her father's people wouldn't care what the Faerians did to her. In fact, she half expected they traded her to the crazed women to be rid of the last of her cursed family. How else would the heretics have known where her hunting ground was located? Or that she'd be there following the buck migration.

The Faerians ignored her pleas and threats, answering the priestess's words with random exclamations of, "Oh, blessed fairies!" and "Take our Forestter sister. Grant us life!"

Long, drifting branches passed over her, the yellowed leaves falling with each push of the breeze. They hit her chest and hips, and fluttered onto the female heads surrounding her only to tangle in their flowing locks. A tiny giggle mingled amongst the swaying treetops and Paige stiffened in horror. Soon the first laugh was followed by more mischievous sounds, as if a choir of fairies watched the procession. She couldn't see them, but that didn't mean they weren't there and very real.

Paige didn't need to see the ground or the pathway in which they traveled to know what was happening. They took her to the sacred circle, to the fairy ring of the great forest to be sacrificed. The trees gave way to a grassy clearing. A ring of stone pillars created a large circle, each roughly carved and three times as tall as the women. Their towering height imposed as it impressed. The believers carried Paige between two of the pillars.

"At least give me back the clothes you stole from me. Don't send me like this!" she screamed, shaking now that they were drawing to the end of the journey. Everyone knew about the fairy rings, had been warned as children to avoid stepping within the fairy playground. Paige's own grandmother claimed to have come through them when she was a young girl. "At least give me my bow. Have some compassion. Don't send me to the fairy world unarmed."

Paige believed in the possibility of fairies, though she had never seen one for herself. From what she had been told as a child, they were mischievous, somewhat vengeful creatures and they liked nothing more than to play tricks on non-worshippers.

"Oh, blessed fairies, here is our sister!" the priestess called. The woman ordered her lowered and Paige felt the cold chill of a stone altar at her naked back. The flimsy gauze they'd wrapped around her waist like a belt hardly counted as clothing. As the material snagged on the rock, the pin holding it close to her hips dug into her flesh.

Paige struggled to be free. A ring of mushrooms

grew in the center of the stones, so innocuous in appearance that if a person didn't know about their hidden magic they might be tempted to step inside. Was this truly the fairy ring, supposed doorway to fairy realm? The truth was Paige didn't know where the ring would lead. No one did. She doubted even the Faerian priestess knew all the fairy secrets. Her grandmother came through and it wasn't the fairy world she had been living in.

The priestess stood over her as countless hands pinned Paige down. The woman's white gown formed tight to her bodice only to flow in long waves along her waist and hips. The skirt trailed behind her in a long train. Tiny gold flowers were embroidered along the hem. Her followers wore the same outfit, minus the embroidery and train. Long, straight black hair seemed to stir around the priestess's oval face, the thin strands dancing like snakes. The woman lifted a wooden cup she had carried with her from the village.

"Drink of the ambrosia," the priestess urged, her gorgeous brown eyes round and filled with promise. "Taste the nectar of the fairy goddess and feel the pleasures of old magic. Let it take you. Let it show you."

Paige clenched her mouth tight, struggling

violently as fingers pressed into her cheeks to force her teeth apart. The priestess's expression didn't change as she leaned over and slowly poured the cup's contents into her prisoner's mouth. Wherever the liquid touched, tingling erupted, almost burning in its intensity.

Paige tried to resist, spitting the liquid out over her face, but it was too much. She was forced to choke down several gulps or drown. The tingling spread down her throat into her stomach and over her cheeks from where trails of discarded liquid touched her flesh. She tried to resist the alluring magic, but it was as useless as resisting the falling rain.

The instant the cup was empty the Faerian women let go, leaving her free to run. Paige shot up on the altar, ready to bolt into the woods to hide, only to be brought short by a transparent winged creature flying in front of her face. Paige jerked back in fright, sliding her ass on the rough stone. The fairy's gown matched that of the priestess, with the train trailing down past her feet as she fluttered about in the air. The creature's eyes looked too big for her face and her skin glimmered, tinged with pale blues and silvers. Silver threads wove in delicate patterns over her wings. Soon more small beings began to appear to her, each tinted with different shades of nature.

Paige couldn't move. The strange sensation of the ambrosia traveled through her blood, leaving her stomach to conquer her limbs. Even her fingernails and hair seemed to prickle. With each passing second, the fairies became clearer. They flew around the gathered worshipers, perching on their shoulders and heads, completely unseen by those who did not drink. Several pulled at the priestess's hair, combing the locks with their fingers to create the snakelike effect she had noticed earlier.

They buzzed around her and Paige jerked, trying to follow them with her eyes. But, when she looked too quickly, the forest blurred into streaks of impossible colors. The Faerians became excited at Paige's apparent visions.

"What madness is this," Paige whispered, swatting at the pests. The flat of her hand managed to smack one across the body and send it flying. Instantly, the others became enraged and attacked. Though Paige tried to fight them off, they swarmed her, pinching her flesh, pulling the long locks of her red hair and the gauze of her belt, pushing wherever they could touch—along the soles of her feet, her exposed sex, her nose and breasts. Paige grunted, flailing about in an effort to be free. With surprising strength, the fairies slid her ass over the coarse surface of stone toward the center ring. For a moment they held her suspended in the air before tossing her at the ground into the ring of mushrooms.

Paige screamed for salvation, but the only answer she received was the high-pitched screech of fairy laughter and the incessant droning of, "Oh, blessed fairies! Take our sister, grant us life!"

End Excerpt

For a complete, up-to-date booklist, visit www. MichellePillow.com

New York Times & *USA TODAY* Bestselling Author

Michelle loves to travel and try new things, whether it's a paranormal investigation of an old Vaudeville Theatre or climbing Mayan temples in Belize. She believes life is an adventure fueled by copious amounts of coffee.

Newly relocated to the American South, Michelle is involved in various film and documentary projects with her talented director husband. She is mom to a fantastic artist. And she's managed by a dog and cat who make sure she's meeting her deadlines.

For the most part she can be found wearing pajama pants and working in her office. There may or may not be dancing. It's all part of the creative process.

Come say hello! Michelle loves talking with readers on social media!

www.MichellePillow.com

facebook.com/AuthorMichellePillow

twitter.com/michellepillow

instagram.com/michellempillow

bookbub.com/authors/michelle-m-pillow

goodreads.com/Michelle_Pillow

amazon.com/author/michellepillow

youtube.com/michellepillow

pinterest.com/michellepillow

COMPLIMENTARY EXCERPTS

TRY BEFORE YOU BUY!

LILITH ENRAPTURED

BY MICHELLE M. PILLOW

Divinity Warriors Book One

Alternate Reality Romance

Sorin of Firewall lives in a land forever at war. In fact, the Starian men are so busy fighting, their marriage ceremony has been reduced to a "will of the gods" event where they simply pick a woman out of a lineup and claim her as a wife. With women becoming scarce, it's necessary to trade the offworld Divinity Corporation for brides. Duty-bound to attend the ceremony, he has no intention of picking a bride, let alone one from another dimension. That is, until he sees Lilith, the bewitching woman sent by the gods to reward—or punish?—him.

Lilith Enraptured Excerpt

Sorin took several deep breaths, feeling as he did when about to go into battle. Heat filled him as tension worked its way into his limbs. With a single thought, he could will his body to spring into action. He could erase her from the world and end this before it started.

But it was too late. He was lost the moment he'd looked at her, had seen her big blue eyes staring at him in trepidation. No, he was lost before that, when he felt her looking at him, beckoning him with her unwavering gaze to find her in the crowd.

Temptress. Witch.

He willed the desire inside him to go away. It shouldn't have been so strong. He'd relieved himself like he always did, had spilled his seed to ease the lonely ache.

Light from the fireplace shone through the white of her gown, silhouetting the long length of her legs and arms. The linen clung to her shoulders, swooping gently along the curves of her breasts— breasts that would be bare beneath. The tied hands were a new addition to the ceremony, thanks to Sir Aidan's wayward woman, Lady Paige. Sorin's barbaric side found he liked the addition.

Hunger rushed into every limb, lifting his cock beneath the long tunic. He didn't think to hide the reaction. No one would care. It had been so long, so very long, since he'd had a woman in his bed. He suppressed a groan. Soft flesh. Round breasts. Taut nipples. Slick, warm vessel to catch his passion. That certain female smell when he pressed his nose to her sex.

A thought whispered in the back of his mind. Maybe she's different. Maybe she'll be better. Maybe this one will stay.

He cursed the thought. No. She wasn't different. She wasn't better. Sorin had made up his mind long ago. He'd come, he'd look, but he never, ever wanted to find someone. He wasn't meant to have this, or her, or any kind of peace. Sorin was born into a land of war. He was made for it, every piece of him. One of the bloodiest battles in their history happened the very hour his mother gave birth to him.

Some were lucky to find peace in marriage, but not him. Tradition and necessity dictated he come to these ceremonies and try to find someone. He came from a noble line, a position of power, one that demanded he have sons to carry on his family's name. But society could not make him choose. It could not make him step forward and lay claim.

"Mine."

Where did that word come from? It sounded like his voice, booming over the hall to quiet all who watched into stunned silence. It felt like his body refusing to go to his place at the table, instead moving forward with arm uplifted to point at the blonde-haired beauty. But it couldn't be his body or his voice. That would mean he'd just announced his claim. Everyone would have heard it. He couldn't back out once the word was said.

"Sorin?" his younger brother, Ronen, hissed. Like Sorin, Ronen led one of the more renowned armies in all of Staria. Very few would dare to challenge their word or honor and the fact made it even more impossible for Sorin to take back what he'd done.

"Mine," Sorin found himself repeating. Was he possessed? What madness was this? He kept walking toward her. She merely stared at him, those wide, gorgeous eyes capturing his. Straight blonde hair hung long down her back, just as a woman's should.

"Brother?" Ronen questioned. The shock was evident in his voice. Sorin couldn't blame him for the surprise because that very day he'd been instructing Ronen to stay strong and not fall for a woman's pretty face. And what did Sorin do? He claimed a woman with a pretty face.

The hall remained quiet. Sorin stopped before the woman, noting with pleasure that she didn't cringe and fall away from his looming presence. Her strength would serve her well. Years of frustrated desires surged inside him. He couldn't put them off any longer. Deny it as he might, he needed a woman. He would never admit the words out loud. The need was not just for physical release, but for the softness of her, the sweet smell and the temporary relief from the endless fighting that such a creature could bring.

You tried this before, Sorin. Such things are not for you.

Fool.

Idiot.

Weak.

His accusing thoughts infuriated. Reaching for her bound arms, he took hold of the ropes. Not even his condescending inner voice could stop his actions. Sorin held her gaze steady, stating so she couldn't mistake his claim, "You are mine."

For a complete, up-to-date booklist, visit www. MichellePillow.com

TAKING KARRE

BY MICHELLE M. PILLOW

Divinity Warriors Book Four
Alternate Reality Romance

Sir Vidar of Spearhead is too busy guarding the borderlands to bother with the headache of selecting a bride. Ordered to marry by the king, he plans to grab a woman and get back to the warfront, never to think of it again. That is until he meets the alluring Lady Karre with her teasing eyes, lush lips and irresistible ways.

Known by many names, inter-dimensional thief Karre, has only one purpose—take down the company that ruined her life. When her luck runs out and she's caught, Divinity Corporation condemns her to matrimony on a primitive, warrior-filled plane where Karre soon discovers there are worse fates than being prisoner to a man with insatiable appetites.

Before long, days and nights filled with bliss becomes something neither expected, and when Karre is taken, Vidar is forced to confront emotions a battle-hardened warrior never expected to feel.

Taking Karre Prologue Excerpt

Three weeks ago, Dimensional Plane 395, Adult Pleasure Centre VWH
Because right now, in this moment, she was their fantasy.

Karre marched out on stage in red stiletto heels, a slinky dress, big grin and nothing else. She kept tempo with the hard, drumming beat of music. Men hollered, whooping their excitement just to see her. She smiled at them, looking over the crowd of heads. She could make them do anything—beg, buy, steal, kill—because right now, in this moment, she was their fantasy.

Blonde hair piled high on her head, garnished with a string of diamonds and rubies some suitor had given her. It was a sweet trinket, one she might even keep, not that she would remember where the jewels came from. She traveled too much and had more important things on her mind.

Karre turned slowly with her arms raised above her head. The hem of her short dress lifted to just below the curve of her ass. When her back was to the crowd, she bent forward. The cheering grew as the men got a peek of the naked treasure hidden beneath the clinging silver. What did she care if they saw her ass? Her pussy? Her breasts? They were just skin, flesh, a tool like any other. No matter how much they wanted her, they would never be able to touch her.

On this dimensional plane of existence, humans cohabitated with humanoid creatures. The first time Karre saw a vampire sucking on the neck of a shifted werewolf, she'd nearly sprinted out of the room to find her wrist portal to flash out of there to another plane. The portable device looked like a large bracelet to most, but to Karre it was her sole means of survival.

Necessity made her stay where she was. This plane was the easiest to get jewels on without resorting to thievery and the hard, shiny rocks were good for trade in nearly every dimension. Besides, not counting the dancing, being in Dimensional Plane 395 was like taking a vacation. With so many strange and different creatures, they never questioned anything she said and most were focused more on blood-drinking and pleasure-seeking.

Being in a new dimensional plane was like being in your world, but only if had it evolved in a different way. To a point, there were many similarities. Languages, generally, were relatively similar, though for some reason the written word consisted of unfamiliar symbols. Some people looked the same, but were not the same people. Natural disasters and major human events were shared. Weather was the same and each place was still Earth.

"I adore you, Sparkle!" a man yelled. "Marry me!"

Karre turned to look over her shoulder at the crowd and winked. A plethora of large green horns, red flesh, reptile skin, webbed fingers, sharp fangs, and ridged flesh stretched out before her until the mass became a single entity flowing back and forth like a wave.

"I'll take that as a yes," the same voice answered her playful flirting. A rush of similar proposals followed the first, showering her in declarations of love. But she wasn't fool enough to believe them. What they felt wasn't love. It was lust.

Karre knew their adoration for what it was and

used it to fuel her dance. She twirled and wiggled, thrust her ass toward them, drew her hips in seductive circles, only to pause in a sexy pose in time with the music. Slowly, she undressed, peeling the slinky gown off her body. Several lights flashed, illuminating her from various angles, leaving no curve unseen.

Just flesh. Just a means. Just another job. Just another plane and soon a distant memory.

Her smile widened, as she knew this was her last dance, at least for this trip. The cheering rose, but she stopped listening. And then it was over. Karre held still, letting the dying notes find their silence before walking naked from the stage.

"You were wonderful tonight, Sparkle," a new dancer fawned. "The crowd loves you. I was wondering if you'd show me how to—"

"Is he here?" Karre asked, stopping the woman from starting a conversation Karre didn't have time for. It's not like she could tell the truth—that all her dancing skill was someone else's memories uploaded into her brain by a device she'd bartered for on another plane.

"He's in your room," the woman answered, frowning slightly at having her question dismissed.

"And he brought a large case. I think it's full of gifts so you'll consider his suit."

"Perfect," Karre grinned. Taking a long robe the woman held out, she slipped it over her shoulders. "I don't want to be disturbed."

✕

Two weeks ago, Dimensional Plane 154, Stac Lesh Mansion
Because right now, in this moment, she was the help.

Karre stared at her red, curly hair in the liquid-silver reflection wall. It had been pulled into a bun at the nape of her neck. The long skirt of the plain uniform and padded body suit did much to hide her figure under the thick gray wool. An apron, changed every time so much as a spot marred the pristine white, covered high over her chest and low to her knees. With the clothes and makeup to pale her face into an unimpressive mask, no one would look twice in her direction because right now, in this moment, she was the help.

She had expected to keep her head down and do her job for months before coming back into this room. But in putting on the uniform, she became invisible. The rich people she worked for didn't look in her direction twice. Well, that wasn't necessarily true. When the wife was gone, the husband had looked at her more than twice. A big grin showcasing blacked-out teeth and a very inappropriately timed belch had changed his interest quickly.

Karre reached to touch her reflection. Behind her, the rich baby's room spread out like the entrance to a palace. Gilded ceilings etched with clouds, golden rays of light and ridiculously cheerful fat angels stretched above as white marble stretched below. It was cold and unwelcoming and more than any one person deserved.

"Oh, wonderful, finally, help," the rich wife said, sweeping into the room. Karre didn't bother to learn the lady's name. "Rich wife" was much easier to remember. The woman held her child under the arms, away from her chest, as if contact with the baby would somehow ruin her carefully planned outfit. "Which one are you?"

"Brigitte, ma'am."

"Take Cinny," the woman ordered. "Mommy needs time to collect herself."

Karre suppressed her groan of frustration at being interrupted and stood to dutifully take the child. She cradled the poor creature close and walked it toward the crib.

"Sing to Cinny before you put her down," rich wife ordered, standing before the liquid silver as she brushed at her clothes.

Karre stopped walking. Sing? To the gurgling, wiggling mass in her arms?

"Well, Brigitte?"

"Mistress, mistress, let me come in," Karre sang the only childlike-sounding song she could think of at the moment, pausing to clear her throat. "I have the pence if you have a quim."

"What a pretty tune," the woman said. "I've never heard it. What does it mean?"

"My dad sang it to my mom," Karre answered, letting the memories she had uploaded into her mind take over her personality—Brigitte of the Fallen Women, a whore's daughter raised in a brothel, adept at blending into new environments. She left off the word "once" before adding the lie, "I'm not sure what it means."

"Carry on."

"Mistress, mistress, I'm stiff as a pin. I need your..." Karre continued, lowering her voice as the woman left her alone with the gurgling, oblivious child. Stopping, she laid the baby down and said,

"Sorry, kid, it's the only song I knew the words to. But I guess it's all right. I turned out just fine with lots of jewels and pretty things and you're too little to understand what any of it means. You should be more worried about growing up in this place with that mom of yours. Now, if you just be good," she paused and tucked a blanket around the infant's body, "I've got a job to do."

Going back to the wall, Karre again reached for her reflection. She stepped forward, letting the liquid hit her hand. It stung, freezing cold in the warm room. For a moment, she hesitated, glancing back at the gurgling child. She thought about grabbing Cinny and taking the baby with her.

"Sorry, kid," she whispered, "even with that mother, you're better off here."

It was a delicate balance—keeping her purpose in her mind while living out the personality and quirks of another—almost like having two people in her head. Karre's hand met with the wall as she felt around, searching for the device she'd hidden. When her fingers met with a smooth, flat surface, she frowned. Putting a second hand to the wall she became frantic, sliding her palms in wide, searching arcs. Perhaps the adhesive she used had come loose. She bent her knees, crouching as she searched the bottom corner of the liquid reflecting wall. Her fingers were so cold it became hard to feel, but the molecular structure of the liquid kept the silver from trickling down her arms as it remained bonded to itself.

Then, to her great surprise, warmth gripped her. A hand wrapped her wrist and jerked her forward. She was pulled through the wall, feeling the sting of silver before landing on a hard, stone floor. Gasping and shivering, she looked around the secret room. A wall of computing towers lined one side, next to three technicians silently typing away on their holographic keypads.

"Lose something, Brigitte?" a man asked, coming close.

Karre glanced up from the floor, "No, sir. I have nothing to lose."

"You are extraordinary." The man laughed. Her eyes instantly took in the familiar insignia of the Divinity Corporation. "Finally, we meet."

Karre forced a grin she didn't feel, letting him see her blackened teeth. Knowing what she looked like, she couldn't help but wonder at his choice of words. Extraordinary? "I wasn't aware we were destined to meet, sir. How lucky for me."

"I can assure you when I'm done with you, you

won't feel lucky." The man leaned down, studying her face. He had the militant rigidity of a soldier, from the purposeful jerks of his body to the engraved frown lines around his mouth and eyes. His hard gaze bored into her, filling her with cold dread. She, or rather Brigitte, had seen that look in men's eyes before. They were usually the kind to beat a prostitute the second they couldn't get their pricks hard.

"I've heard that one before," she mumbled, pretending to be unimpressed.

"I'm Director Tomes and..." He paused, lifting the small, wrist-wrapping device she'd been searching the liquid-silver wall for. Divinity had the only known source of top-secret inter-dimensional travel technology and they wouldn't like the fact that someone had stolen it. "I have a feeling you know where I am from. It was very naughty of you to borrow our only portable jump prototype. Our scientists will be very interested in seeing how you got it to work. This device will make traveling to uncharted worlds much easier. No more carting around temporary portals. No more perfectly timed pickups from headquarters. No more rescue parties."

Less supervision so you can do more dark deeds, Karre silently added.

"We'll be able to explore planes at a much faster rate," Tomes continued, as if it was a good thing.

Just like an infectious disease.

"Sorry, I'm not available for science lessons, but if you'd like to make an appointment, I'm sure I can fit you in," Karre hummed in pretend thought, "uh, never."

"Oh, you're going to be fun to break, my dear," Tomes promised. "Talbert. Get her ready to go."

For a complete, up-to-date booklist, visit www. MichellePillow.com

BARBARIAN PRINCE

BY MICHELLE M. PILLOW

Dragon Lords Series

Bestselling Shapeshifter Romance

Breaking up was never so hard...

Going undercover at a mass wedding as a bartered bride, Morrigan Blake has every intention of getting off the barbaric planet just as soon as it's over. Or, more correctly, just as soon as she captures footage of the mysterious princes rumored to be in attendance.

But after a euphoric night, Morrigan discovers her ride left without her, and Ualan of Draig is claiming she's his wife. It's not exactly the story this reporter had in mind. And to make matters worse, the all-to-seductive alpha refuses to take no for an answer.

Being cursed by the gods was never so frustrating...

Prince Ualan is prepared to follow dragonshifter tradition and marry the woman revealed to him during the Breeding Festival. When the stubborn, yet achingly sexy, Morrigan refuses to accept their shared fate and his supreme authority over her, it is all he can do to keep from acting like the barbarian she accuses him of being.

For a complete, up-to-date booklist, visit www. MichellePillow.com

Printed in Great Britain
by Amazon